CUTHBERT
How Mean is my Valley

#2

by

Patrick Barrett

A Wild Wolf Publication

Published by Wild Wolf Publishing in 2016
Copyright © 2016 Patrick Barrett

ISBN: 978-1-907954-51-1
Also available as an e-book

www.wildwolfpublishing.com

I am dedicating the second book in the Cuthbert series to my beautiful wife, Paula Jayne, without whom these books would never have seen the light of day.

Chapter One

The Valley usually awoke to the sound of a cock crowing, but if the crow couldn't find him, the Valley folk would hear his poor impersonation instead.

This particular morning, Percy was shaken awake as his shed vibrated around him. He opened one eye to see a row of plant-pots dancing along his shelf and a large green leafy thing in a pot jitterbugging in the corner. His 'gardening trophies' bought from charity shops and with the sporting bits snapped off, had formed an orderly queue at one end of the shelf and were jumping off in pairs like a parachuting display team.

Percy, according to rumours he had spread himself, had been the gardener at Mandrake Hall. The Hall was no longer in existence after a disastrous fire during one of the lapses of sanity which seemed to afflict the Valley from time to time.

Jamming on his hat, Percy swung out of his makeshift bed, slamming both feet hard against the cold floor.

This was unheard of as Percy's turned down wellies were always positioned precisely so that he could leave his shed in an emergency ready equipped for any amount of gardening crises.

Retrieving them from against the far wall, he synchronised his hopping with the plant in the corner and they fell out of the door together.

Chapter Two

A small hill just behind the shed had always hidden the Hall from view and Percy stood and stared at its crest.

A sudden roaring noise and a huge plume of smoke added to the confusion of images assailing Percy when he really wasn't at his best. He stumbled to the top of the hill and stared again.

Below him, several huge, bright yellow monsters spewed oily black smoke as they lumbered into formation; huge blades at the front of the machines dropped in unison and the diggers roared together as they folded up the earth before them and pushed it ahead. Percy was appalled. They were tearing up the foundations of Mandrake Hall and, in theory at least, jeopardising his invented livelihood.

Percy spun on his heel and went to fetch help; at least, that was the message he sent to his feet. What actually happened was that in his hurry, he had put one welly on backwards and as he spun, he tripped and rolled straight down the hill towards the earth movers, seeing alternate flashes of sky, grass and imminent death, all accompanied by the symphony of clutches, gears and clanking tracks.

Percy rolled himself into a ball at the bottom of the hill and awaited his fate. Finding himself being rolled up like Cleopatra in a grass carpet, he broke away and ran straight into the path of another earth mover. Taking immediate evasive action, he careered around one huge blade and narrowly missed another. He now felt like the shiny ball in a pinball machine.

All around him, the machines poured smoke from pipes with flaps on the top which seemed to be laughing at him as they opened and closed. Percy felt himself being rolled up again and he jumped up and grabbed onto the top rim of the excavator's blade. Clinging on for dear life, Percy stared into the eyes of the driver.

The man opened his mouth in a silent scream and pushed, pulled and kicked several levers at once. The gigantic machine lurched sideways, spinning on one track until its blade collided with another one working alongside.

Percy was thrown off and rolled clear as a resounding clang sounded above all else. Percy looked around carefully; the sudden silence made him suspicious. He was surrounded by boots - big, muddy boots all connected to big muddy legs and huge belt buckles.

"What is it?" asked a voice. "A Hobbit?"

"Don't know," said another. "Frightened me to death."

Percy felt himself being picked up by his jacket and dumped back upright.

"He's got funny feet," observed the owner of one voice.

"It's a Hobbit, then," declared another.

Percy spat out a lump of mud and spluttered, "I am not a Hobbit. I am the Gardener at the Hall." He glared defiantly.

"What Hall?" someone retorted.

"This Hall!" yelled Percy waving an arm at the desolation around him.

"Concussed Hobbit?" suggested someone.

"Got all the hallmarks," said another dryly.

This caused a laugh and everyone lost interest and started to climb back into the machines. Percy just gaped around him and shouted, "Who is in charge?"

One of the men pointed to a rectangular building which hadn't been there yesterday and Percy scuttled out of the way as the roaring, clanking and crunching began again. Two of the giant beasts seemed to be stuck together and a group of large men in yellow plastic helmets began to gather around it.

Percy stomped up the steps and banged on the door of this building marked 'Office'. After banging twice, Percy threw open the door and stormed in. The place had carpets, a desk, computers and curtains. It was better than Percy's shed.

A door opened in the far wall and out stepped a thing of beauty; casually flicking back her long blonde hair, the woman neatly held it in place by pressing a yellow helmet over it.

"Oh, I'm sorry, I didn't hear you," she purred as Percy melted and tried to slick his hair down with mud. "I am the Site Manager. Can I help?"

A walkie-talkie device on the desk crackled into life and with a smile at Percy, she moved and picked it up. Studying Percy as if he were an escaped lab- rat, she muttered responses into the device and then set it down again.

"Well," she began, "it seems that you have tangled two very expensive machines together. Have you come to apologise?"

Percy was still trying to reconcile the shape of her overalls compared to the men outside and he was caught wrong-footed.

"Apologise, me, apologise?" he spluttered as her words registered. "Why … "

She interrupted as smooth as tearing satin, and purred, "It's alright, we realised that when we came to backward parts we would cause quite a culture shock. We won't say anymore about it." She pursed her lips as if blowing him a kiss. This caused him to step back and she closed the door behind him.

Percy stood outside the Portacabin in shock. All he held dear had been threatened and almost separated from the rest of him and he hadn't said a word. These women, he thought, once they fell for you, they could beguile you in an instant.

Chapter Three

Starting to walk across the rutted mud, Percy's eye was drawn to
something bobbing up and down in the smoke above one of the
machines - his hat. Clambering furiously onto the machine, he snatched
his hat and ran towards the farm.

"CUTHBERT," he yelled.

Cuthbert and the crow saw him coming. The crow somehow
managed to shrug under its feathers and show Cuthbert its sympathetic
side.

Percy was bouncing from side to side as he ran and one of his
wellies was trying to face the same direction as its mate, acting as a
rudder and causing him to veer off course. He ricocheted off the barn
wall and pausing to re-aim, set off again, arms flailing like a
semaphore tower in a gale.

Cuthbert was tempted to wait until the last moment and
nonchalantly close the door between them, but the sulking would go on
for days. Besides, Cuthbert was mildly curious.

Percy, collapsed on his knees, panting like a ruptured steam boiler
- his only method of communication left - seemed to be pointing. So he
pointed to Cuthbert, pointed to himself and then to the horizon.

Cuthbert mischievously suggested, "You wish you were me
because you could go far?"

Percy shook his head wildly and mimicked a man digging a hole.

"You've come about the grave-digger's position?" Cuthbert was
enjoying this.

Percy glared at him and tried flapping one hand up and down on
top of his head and pushing the other hand forward to show the action
of the earth-movers.

Cuthbert tried, "Big chief want pow-wow with little chief to push
white man back across river, eh? No wonder you're panicking."

The crow simply sat there with its beak open. They called him
'bird-brain', yet look at this pair.

Percy made a gigantic effort, but the attempt came out as a garbled
whooshing noise.

"Oh, I see," said Cuthbert in sudden enlightenment. "The
earthmovers have arrived and they are digging new foundations at the

site of the old hall. Why didn't you say so?" With that, he stepped into the house and closed the door.

Cuthbert waited inside, and suddenly the door shook, one corner after the other, top and bottom alternatively.

Sunlight flashed through the gaps in the planks as they heaved apart under the blows. Cuthbert had visions of Percy levitating in mid-air and using all his limbs at once. Maybe, this was something he had learnt from the legendary 'Tsun-Beam' at some time during his incredibly complicated past.

The banging stopped and the dust settled. Cuthbert opened the door to see Percy in the stance of the fighting bull, nostrils flaring and chest heaving.

"Cup of tea?" asked Cuthbert sweetly.

They sat opposite each other across the farmhouse table. Bits kept falling off Percy as the mud dried, and Cuthbert imagined himself having tea with the Lepers' Guild.

"You knew," accused Percy as an exact mould of his nose fell off.

"Why didn't you tell me?" he continued. "I only just escaped. That woman was obsessed with me."

Cuthbert wondered which bit would fall off next and whether it would affect the woman's obsession at all. "The letter came two days ago and you were off sulking somewhere," explained Cuthbert patiently.

"I don't sulk," snapped Percy, before asking, "What letter?"

Cuthbert explained that the old family firm of solicitors had written to him to warn him of the sale of the old Hall site.

It assured him that his farm and its outbuildings were not involved and he was not to worry, so he hadn't.

"Who bought it?" Percy asked, sipping his tea.

"Some firm called 'Cash-Go' supermarkets," replied Cuthbert.

"Hmm, wonder if they'll need a gardener?' Percy mused and promptly left to see if his new admirer had any vacancies.

Chapter Four

Cuthbert washed the cups and stared vacantly out of his window; he saw Percy galloping back towards him over the hill, bouncing off the barn and flailing towards the door again.

'Better make up the spare bed,' thought Cuthbert. 'Percy's shed used to be on the land bought by Cash-Go.'

Change didn't come easily to the Valley. The population was split between newcomers and 'old Valley folk.'

Cuthbert was old Valley thanks to his mother, and the fact that he upheld the theatrical passions of the Valley.

It had long been believed that a young William Shakespeare had worked at Mandrake Hall as a teacher. There were even old scrolls surviving which suggested that he had begun writing his plays whilst in the Valley.

Many of the old Valley inhabitants had middle names taken from his plays as an act of homage, or in the case of Billy 'Bottom' Whyper, an act of crass stupidity. Billy was the Valley's odd-job man, so called because his repair work was decidedly odd.

Some of his solutions were breath-taking, like the wind turbine he fitted to the quaint old 'Lower cottage'. He used the sails from the old windmill and every time the wind howled up the Valley, 'Lower cottage' moved about three yards East.

It had already been re-named 'Middle cottage,' and was now known as 'Top Cottage'. The postman had refused to deliver, until they 'Stopped messing about.'

Several newcomers had been grudgingly accepted recently. Henry Chisholm had once travelled the world as a news presenter but had settled down to marry Margery. They had bought the Mandrake Arms Public House and packed the terrible twins off to boarding school. The twins were due home anytime while the chemistry block was being rebuilt.

Henry's quaintly homicidal brother, Ronald, was abroad, testing guns for the military. He was the subject of an enquiry. Apparently, he had never used up his allocation of paper targets but he was always short of native assistants.

Henry's daughter, affectionately known as Arkle due to a family resemblance to the famous racehorse, was traveling the world with Geraldine, the museum curator. They had both escaped from a mental asylum, but as the Valley rightly knew, "It was all a bit of a misunderstanding."

Captain Edgar and Elspeth had stayed on at the Mill and they lived peacefully. He was writing military histories and she was defying any dust to cross her threshold.

Incidentally, the whole area was criss-crossed with ancient and recent tunnel systems linking houses and churches and halls and crypts, and even Cuthbert's cellar. No-one really had to get wet when it rained in the Valley, but it was always polite to knock.

Cuthbert, of course, was the local undertaker. He ran his business from one of many out-buildings and now he seemed to have an apprentice.

Percy had moved in with him and was endlessly fascinated by every process involved in hiding relatives before they began to smell. Cuthbert was carefully sewing various bits of farmer Griffin back together after his combine harvester accident, when Percy appeared at his shoulder.

"Using that stitch are you?" he began, shuffling to get comfortable on the edge of the slab. This was a bad sign and Cuthbert prepared himself for more.

"One of my ancestors did all Nelson's sewing," he said, eyeing Cuthbert's neat workmanship. "Sewed his empty sleeve up to his shoulder, she did, and stopped it flapping in the wind. Everybody wondered why the sailors kept running up and down the rigging when it was windy. They thought he was giving instructions." Percy paused and noticed that Cuthbert's line of stitching wasn't as straight as it had been, so he continued.

"Sewed his eyelid shut as well, after he lost his eye." He paused. "Remember that famous quote, 'I see no ships', when he disobeyed an order and held the telescope to his blind eye?"

Cuthbert nodded despite himself.

"What he actually said was, 'I see no ships. That bloody woman's sewed the wrong eye up'."

Cuthbert's lips were trembling and his hand was shaking but he soldiered on.

11

Percy watched the stitches getting sloppy and said, "She sewed all his battle flags as well, you know. When they signalled the fleet at Trafalgar, she had used up all her thread patching Nelson up, and she had nicked several signal flags and cut them up for hangings around his cot, so, all they could send was, 'England expects you to give them a good licking'. Now, some of those lads had been at sea for some time. It's no wonder they won."

Cuthbert gave up. The needle had gone through farmer Griffin's nose and he had sewn one of the arms to his own jacket.

"Cup of tea?" asked Percy innocently.

Chapter Five

The atmosphere in the snug was tense. Everyone had gathered to air their views on the new supermarket. People were suddenly concerned about their quality of life and some of them realised that they had never had any.

Henry took over and called the meeting to order. His wife, Margery, watched him fondly, and Belinda was outside watching odd-job Billy putting planks over the windows, ready for the return of the twins.

Henry cleared his throat. "My main concern," he began, "is that we were not consulted about this development at all. No-one seems to know who owned the Hall or even how it became separated from the farm in the first place."

An arched eyebrow was aimed at Cuthbert but was met by a blank stare. Cuthbert had been told by his late parents that everything was taken care of and he mustn't worry, so, he hadn't.

Every now and then the old family firm of solicitors would send him a letter explaining all recent developments, and at the bottom it always said that he was not to worry. After a while he skipped most of the letter and went straight to the bottom to check his standing instruction. As long as it said that he was not to worry, Cuthbert happily complied.

Percy wasn't sitting with Cuthbert. He had started off at the back, giving out deep sighs as befitted a man just made homeless in an act of desecration. After a short interval of being completely unnoticed, he moved forward and tried again. The problem was that half the Valley didn't know who he was and the other half never knew where he lived anyway, so, in the end he sat quietly in a very menacing manner.

Henry had spoken to the Head Office of Cash-Go supermarkets and discovered that this was to be their biggest development to date. If he understood the figures given to him for 'Retail Area Floor Space', they may as well simply put a roof over the whole Valley! This drew gasps from the audience and a panic attack from Mrs. Biggle, the Post Mistress, who wondered how the telegrams would be delivered if the pigeons couldn't get out. A tinkling laugh from the back caused everyone to jerk around simultaneously like puppets with tangled strings.

The vision Percy had encountered sashayed down the aisle to the front where Henry automatically stepped aside for her.

Pausing, to remove her yellow plastic helmet, the newcomer swung her head to one side, and a sheen of pure blonde hair swept first one way and then the other, before settling like a cloak across her shoulders. She smiled. Adoration radiated from the men in the audience and pure molten animosity oozed from the women; the newcomer had their attention.

"My name is Anita," she purred, "Anita Peace."

The men mentally juggled with images and anagrams and generally enjoyed the show. The women watched like coiled snakes as Anita explained that the development would bring prosperity to the Valley and create many local jobs, freeing them from the mediaeval clutches of their evil landowner.

This last remark was addressed directly at Cuthbert, and the whole room turned to stare at him. Cuthbert was a seasoned performer, and in panic, shock or fear, he gave nothing away. However, his mind was travelling like a hamster in a wheel, to about the same effect.

Anita purred gently and attention returned to the front, giving Cuthbert a breathing space just as panic and confusion were causing the little hamster's feet to smoke. Anita held up a slim, delicate wrist and all could see a glitteringly expensive watch with a square face.

"What does this symbolise?" she asked dramatically. All faces were turned to her now.

"Oh, oh, I know this one," shouted Percy, jumping up and down. "Women wear square watches so that time can hide in the corners and then they can pretend they don't know where it's gone." He sat stiffly upright, beaming like the school sneak revealing the broken window.

Apparently, the women still had a supply of venom left, and Percy slowly sank down in his chair trying to minimise his neck as if he were queuing for the guillotine.

Cuthbert watched his new friend's discomfort 'At least, I'll still have someone to talk to,' he thought gratefully.

"Time," announced Anita, "it symbolises time. Times are changing - it's time to be free. The rest of the country doesn't get its hands dirty pulling up potatoes, scrubbing them, peeling them and then bashing them to bits so that his Lordship can leave them on the edge of his plate and go for a pint." She had them now. The women were on the edge of their seats and the men's eyes were sliding sideways in alarm.

The rhetoric continued. Someone was a capitalist lackey, someone else was a retarded Neanderthal and there were apparently loads of repressive ignoramuses in the Valley.

The men didn't know who was who but they were certain that they were all in there somewhere.

The milkman, and regular leading man in all the Valley's theatre productions, struck his most heroic pose to date. "What about my milk round?" he boomed. "What about my business?"

The crowd nodded sympathetically.

Anita intervened silkily. "Your business?" she purred. "Isn't it our business when you clatter into the cobbled street, shattering the sleep of law-abiding residents, clanking glass bottles about and whistling?" She paused for effect and pointed a finger at the stricken man. "And is it our business how you treat that magnificent example of equus domesticus?" she screamed.

Silence followed, until someone added helpfully, "His horse."

"Ahh," sighed the crowd.

The milkman slammed down into his seat. He wasn't just in the guillotine queue; he could hear the swish of the blade.

"Think of it, ladies," continued Anita. "If you have really got to feed him, you don't have to go out and kill it first. Simply rip its top off and microwave it."

The men were trying to sidle out into the bar as the sounds of women's revolutionary chanting took hold, but a chill seemed to descend upon the room.

"And now I will introduce you to the person responsible for your freedom, ladies." Her eyes glowed with revolutionary fervour as she swept an arm towards the door.

The double doors were flung wide open and the people of the Valley gasped. Against a backdrop of smoke from Old Charlie's bonfire, a woman with hair of fire rode silently into the room on an electric mobility scooter. She came slowly between the rows of people, taking in the scene on either side of her with a calculating, soul-searching stare. Slowly circling the table where Anita stood in rapture, she pulled up to face her audience.

15

After a calculated pause, she flicked a long strand of Titian hair back over her shoulder and spoke. "I am the owner of Cash-Go supermarkets." Looking straight at Cuthbert, she inclined her head. "It's good to see you again, Cuthbert." Causing another mass marionette moment, she swept the room with her green eyes and declared, "Some call me Red."

Chapter Six

Cuthbert was stunned. He sat at his kitchen table with solicitor's letters strewn all around him. It was all there - the enquiries, the proposals, the acceptance and enough Don't Worries to fill a diplomatic corps' in-tray.

Percy sat opposite, eyes like saucers, thanks to a pair of circular spectacles perched on his nose.

"Where did you get those?" Cuthbert asked, giving shock and surprise a moment to relax.

"That box over there," Percy answered vaguely with a wave of his arm. "Collect them, do you?"

Cuthbert sighed and replied, "Only when they don't need to be buried with the deceased. Those were Mr. Hinges'."

Percy's huge eyes swam for a moment as he tried to shift from the letter and re-focus on Cuthbert. "No wonder he stepped in front of a bus," Percy muttered.

After a while, Percy set down the letter, removed Mr. Hinges' shop windows and peered hard at Cuthbert. "So, basically," he began, "your family has owned Mandrake Hall, and the farm, and the old mill for quite a while and you are as rich as creosote?"

Rubbing the bridge of his nose, Percy began to pace up and down as if he were at the Old Bailey. Sticking his thumbs into his waistcoat buttonholes, he muttered something about pro bono and Corpus Christi, followed by 'veritas, varieties', and even began wagging his finger at an imaginary jury.

"Got some experience in this field, have we?" asked Cuthbert dryly.

Percy span around and pointed directly at Cuthbert. "You may mock, sirrah, but this is a classic case of the little man being forced to triumph against the mighty corporations. This is my chance to reduce the legislative footprint of these fiendish fanatics."

Cuthbert was fascinated. It only needed a clap of thunder and Percy would be handing out stone tablets. "So, you would help me to throw off these capitalist shackles and regain my standing in the Valley?" Cuthbert asked admiringly.

"What? Er … no," Percy stammered. "I was talking about suing you and getting a new shed."

Late into the night, Cuthbert sat with his head on his arms, thinking back to the snatches of conversations he had heard between his parents. His mother had often referred to her 'paper fortune' and this must have been it. They didn't need to be real Valley folk - they owned the real Valley.

Chapter Seven

Even the crow was taken by surprise the next morning. He managed one quick squawk and flew into the chimney stack.

Cuthbert was still at the kitchen table with his head on his arms. A grinding crash of gears outside caused his head to jerk up suddenly, biting the button off his cuff as he did so.

Percy flew downstairs, hit the banister rail where the stairs turned, and somersaulted into the other half of the house.

Cuthbert dashed to the door, tore it open and was faced with a wall of soil and rocks, and it was coming towards him.

Hearing Percy somewhere behind him, Cuthbert turned and opened his mouth to shout a warning, but the percussive qualities of the capital 'P' caused the button to fly straight as an arrow, hitting Percy between the eyes and knocking him straight onto his back.

Turning back to the door, Cuthbert was hit in the face by the wall of soil and pushed steadily backwards until he fell over the prostrate form of Percy at the bottom of the stairs.

They lay together in a tangle of limbs as the house darkened and then started to become light again. The soil retreated and the sunlight streamed in. Silhouetted in the doorway was a seated figure, hair shining like a halo of fire.

"Morning, boys. Hope I haven't interrupted anything," cried the figure gliding silently towards them.

Cuthbert and Percy battled to untangle themselves in as masculine a way as possible and stood abashed before her, wondering why they appeared to be in the wrong. Cuthbert remembered the wall of soil and, dashing to the door, saw a bulldozer sat there like a bulldog straining at its leash and panting to have another go.

"What's happening?" he managed.

"Silly boy," said the woman on the scooter. "I could hardly live here without a ramp to the front door now, could I?"

"Live here?" spluttered Cuthbert. "But we live here." It didn't sound right even as he said it but Cuthbert was reeling from shock.

"And who is this charming little playmate of yours?" she asked.

Percy stood simpering like a wet spaniel, and for a moment Cuthbert thought that he was going to curtsey - that would really put the cherry on top.

"He's not my playm ... " A loud bell clanged at the back of Cuthbert's brain. "Playmate." As soon as the clanging stopped, he could hear the thought. "Aunt Liza," he breathed.

"Of course it is, dear, who else would it be?" she replied. "Good grief, why have you still got that?" she asked, nodding at the Grandfather clock. Cuthbert could have sworn the clock was ticking faster in panic. "Never mind, all in good time, everything comes out in the wash."

The scooter was already gliding eerily into the next room and something crashed back against the wall.

"You're not much help," Cuthbert snapped.

Percy looked dreamily after Aunt Liza and said, "What do I tell the blonde, now this one has fallen for me?"

Cuthbert pushed past him and went to rescue his possessions from the wheels of doom.

Outside, the bulldozer had made new roads and wider pathways to each of Cuthbert's out-buildings and barns, and was merrily heading towards the village like a snow plough with a faulty calendar.

Anita Peace, the site foreman, met them outside after striding across the mounds of soil and mud. Glancing at Cuthbert and Percy for a moment, she addressed Liza. "That's the farm complex done, boss. We're just linking you to the village now. The hardcore is on its way."

Liza beamed her thanks and they all set off to test how level the roadways were. "Is that condemned?" asked Liza, pointing to the huge barn with its 'Soweto' style additions.

"That's the theatre," said Anita with a smirk.

"Oh good Lord," muttered Liza, speeding away in front.

Percy had been trying to catch Anita's eye for some time as they walked so that he could let her down gently, but as she strode ahead, Percy was skipping to catch up and the newly turned mud on his boots wasn't helping at all.

He watched Anita stride through another puddle of sludge, with her boots still looking brand new, and he was stammering something inaudible as he rehearsed his speech.

"Oh for goodness sake, Percy," fumed Cuthbert. "Stop her and say it."

"Say what?" enquired Anita, turning and fixing Percy with a glare.

"Oh er ... er ..." stumbled Percy. "Are those Teflon wellies?"

Liza had entered through a side door, and now the two main doors flew open as she rammed them apart for the others to enter.

They all stood in silence, Cuthbert in silent pride. The two women stood in stupefied amazement, and Percy in astonishment, at the improvements in welly technology.

Anita laughed out loud, "This won't stand a chance against the Cin ... " she faltered, catching her boss' eye.

"Sin?" asked Cuthbert, "What sin?"

"Nothing, just a technical word," she said trying to keep a straight face. "Oh, that reminds me, boss, there's a delay with the rows of seats."

Liza nodded absently before pointing to the front row and asking "Is that a tractor seat?"

Chapter Eight

Sitting at the kitchen table later that day, Cuthbert and Percy tried to make sense of what had happened.

"What I don't understand," said Percy, "is how all the mud slides off. Real advance in gardening technology, that is. Next they will be making insects attack each other and grass made of plastic, if you ask me."

Cuthbert didn't ask him. He was puzzled. Wouldn't stand a chance against what sin? Why does a supermarket need rows of seats? "Percy," he began, "I need your help."

Percy picked himself up off the floor and looked suspicious. "Really?" he asked.

Cuthbert was in super-serious mood and he began with, "What could they be building that begins with sin?"

"Supermarket," suggested Percy.

"Sin," prompted Cuthbert patiently.

"Single-storey supermarket," said Percy eagerly, starting to enjoy this game.

Cuthbert gave Percy the stare he reserved for customers who wanted a relative exhumed to see if he had done a good job before they paid, and Percy took the hint.

"Singles bar," he tried, "sing-song, sing-a-long bar." Scratching his head under his cap, he came up with, "Singed couples' therapy centre."

"Where on earth do you spend your time?" asked Cuthbert in exasperation.

Percy sat right on the edge of a good sulk and muttered, "Used to watch the adverts when my Dad was a projectionist."

Cuthbert looked surprised for a moment. "I didn't know your Dad was a projectionist."

Percy brightened immediately and Cuthbert realised his mistake. Too late now, grin and bear it, he thought.

Percy shuffled to get comfortable and Cuthbert groaned.

"Oh yes, my Dad was a pioneer. He tried to revolutionise the world of projection," said Percy proudly.

"Tried to project his methods worldwide, did he? Cuthbert asked to no avail.

Percy ploughed on regardless. "He was incredible at winding the handle at just the right speed, was my Dad. If the action speeded up a bit, you knew he was running late and Mum had his dinner ready." He paused to make sure that Cuthbert was paying attention and continued. "He was never happy after they automated things and he had to wait for the film to finish and let his dinner get cold. He used to sit at the table and count the gravy-rings left when everything congealed, and Mum would make sure he still ate it, slice by slice."

Another check on Cuthbert's awareness before he carried on.

"Anyway, he realised that the speed of the film now depended on gears driving sprockets which fitted into loads of square holes down each side of the film. This meant they could only watch three films a day and dad was eating sliced gravy again." He watched Cuthbert very closely, just in case he had embalmed his own eyelids while no-one was looking, and carried on.

"The Royal Family was coming on this particular day to see the first filmed coronation ever and Dad saw an opportunity to be famous. Everybody wanted to see the film and they were prepared to pay more on the first day, so Dad sat on the projection room floor with a pair of scissors and joined all the perforations up. This meant that he could pull the film through by hand and have eight showings a day instead of three."

There was no doubt at all about Cuthbert's attention at this point, he was hooked.

"The great day arrived," Percy continued, "the Royal Family took their seats, and the music began. Unfortunately, the gears didn't just move the film, they also pulled it tight and kept the celluloid away from the very hot bulb. Well, Dad was pulling at a fair rate of knots when he sneezed due to the celluloid dust from cutting the film. The film went slack and caught fire. Dad pulled faster to put the fire out, the 'Keystone cops' coronation shot out of the front and a three foot flame shot out of the back. The tripod collapsed and the rest of the film was shown on the back of the King's bald head."

Percy waited proudly for the reaction but even he was amazed when Cuthbert jumped to his feet and cried, "That's it!"

"Er, no it's not. Dad proved that it didn't work," he said, watching his friend clenching his fists and changing colour.

Cuthbert slammed his fist down on the table, making Percy's hat jump. "You've solved it," he yelled.

"I have?" replied Percy, trying hard to take the credit but failing miserably.

Cuthbert fixed him with a manic stare. "What makes everybody face forward and uses lots of seats?"

Percy tried but Cuthbert's glare was rather disconcerting, "A train, a tram, a bus … " he tried desperately.

Cuthbert thumped the table again and Percy stopped guessing.

"A cinema," said Cuthbert, loathing dripping from every syllable. "We have a theatre and they want to show ELECTRIC PEOPLE."

"Oh," said Percy.

Chapter Nine

No-one slept very much that night. Cuthbert could be heard pacing up and down, shouting to the rafters and ranting at the world in general.

Waking next morning to the sounds of drilling and hammering downstairs, he ran to the top of the stairs to see what the blazes Percy was doing now.

Percy had been downstairs making breakfast for his friend and was heading back to the stairs when the noise started.

Cuthbert stormed onto the stairs to find three workmen fitting a stair-lift from top to bottom, screwing straight into the ancient timber.

"Enough is enough," he roared, standing squarely on the bend in the stairs and refusing to move.

The workmen ignored him and carried on around him. One even put a large screw through the bottom of his pajama leg as he stood there.

Percy moved towards the bottom step with a tray full of cups and toast just as the door burst inwards with a crash. Percy dropped the tray and jumped up.

Cuthbert jumped out of his pyjama bottoms and fell on top of Percy as they ended once more in a tangle at the bottom of the stairs.

"Oh boys, there will have to be more discipline after I move in, you know," said Aunt Liza as she surveyed the tangle before gliding into the kitchen.

Huge trucks rumbled through the farm and the village all the rest of that day.

When Cuthbert and Percy stepped outside, all the newly flattened roads had been coated with light coloured hard-core and flattened again.

Percy thought it was great and he went off bouncing from side to side, singing, "Dum-de-dum, De-dum-de-dum, follow the yellow brick road." Cuthbert watched him go and marvelled at how little it took to keep Percy amused.

While going through the village, Cuthbert began to notice that every house and shop now had the road leading to their doors and it was graded into a ramp at each one.

Percy had reappeared at his side and Cuthbert pointed it out.

"Marvellous," said Percy emphatically.

"What is?" asked Cuthbert.

"Ramps," said Percy. "Every gardener appreciates ramps. Bring a wheelbarrow right into the house with ramps."

Cuthbert walked on steadily, still grumpy as he asked, "Why would anyone do that?"

Percy gave Cuthbert the sympathetic look reserved for morons and non-gardeners, and said, "Indoor plants," as he skipped along happily beside Cuthbert.

Cuthbert opened his mouth to ask, but Percy stopped suddenly and looked at his companion in sheer amazement. "You don't know, do you?"

"Know what?" asked Cuthbert suspiciously.

Percy never took his eyes off Cuthbert as he shook his head in wonderment. "Did you really think that the plants hide under the soil in winter and then simply pop up again in spring? Unbelievable."

"Well," said Cuthbert indignantly, "I did rather think that, yes."

Percy sniggered. "Silly boy. We take them all inside and then bring them back out again. It will be early flowering this spring, you just watch."

"Why's that?" asked Cuthbert, bemused.

Percy was still shaking his head at him. "Ramps. Were you not listening?"

Any reply Cuthbert may have conjured up was lost by a sudden impression of speed - a blur and an ungentle nudge into the ditch.

Picking himself up, Cuthbert looked at Percy who was scratching his head admiringly as Aunt Liza zoomed silently towards the village, long red hair flying behind her.

"Look at her go," he said. "Like Basil Brush on speed."

Chapter Ten

The Mandrake Arms was almost full but the customers were subdued. The twins were due back today and the Valley was only just realising what peace was.

Everyone looked up at the sound of a taxi outside and the atmosphere crackled with tension. The door opened in a smooth, controlled motion, and there they were.

The men at the tables slowly lifted both feet off the floor while putting one hand on their wallets and raising each glass clear of the table top. Old habits died hard.

Everyone gaped. Into the room strode two young men wearing immaculate slacks, blazers and straw boaters.

"Hello, Mater," said one twin.

"Hello, Mater and step-Pater," said the other twin.

They simultaneously doffed their hats to the assembly, placed vintage leather cases on the floor and moved to shake hands with their mother.

Margery was choked with emotion and she swept them into a back room to welcome them home in style.

The majority of the customers were relieved.

Percy was remembering past humiliations and Cuthbert was appalled; he had rather hoped to utilise the twins and their knowledge of guerrilla tactics in his battle against the cinema.

The twins reappeared after a while and began to help around the bar, clearing glasses, wiping tables and calling everyone 'Sir.'

Cuthbert was suspicious; leopards might change their spots but they still got hungry.

He sidled up to one of the twins. "Fond memories, eh?" he asked.

The twin looked steadily at him and replied, "I am sorry, sir, I don't understand the allusion."

Neither did Cuthbert but he continued. "Come on, all the mischief. You could write a book."

The twin brightened visibly and Cuthbert thought, 'This is better. Now we're getting somewhere.'

The twin casually doffed his straw boater as Belinda passed and addressed Cuthbert. "I have actually just completed a translation of

Homer's Odyssey into Aramaic. Apparently schools in the desert regions cannot always obtain such fine works." He looked at Cuthbert as if daring him to challenge such noble ideals.

Cuthbert looked over the twin's shoulder and said, "Don't look now but old Charlie has nodded off with his pipe in his pocket and his jacket is smouldering. Wonder if his teeth will melt this time."

The twin whipped around, grabbed a soda-siphon, extinguished the pocket blaze, pushed Charlie's dentures back in and wiped the table all in one fluid motion. "Thank you, sir," he said. "Between us we have averted quite a catastrophe."

Then he walked away.

Cuthbert was ecstatic. The actions had been instinctive, the motions smooth, but Cuthbert had seen it. Just for a millisecond the guard had dropped and it had escaped - a flash of mischief.

As the twin reached the far end of the bar, Cuthbert asked loudly, "So we beat you, then?"

The twin paused.

Cuthbert continued. "Percy always said you were no match for him."

The air between them whistled and the wall behind Cuthbert vibrated. Cuthbert turned, and there, stuck deep into an ancient wooden beam by its specially sharpened rim, was a straw boater.

Cuthbert smiled. The twins were back.

Chapter Eleven

Cuthbert sat alone in a corner, his drink untouched.

He usually confided in Belinda, the barmaid, but lately she seemed pre-occupied and didn't stay in one place behind the bar for long.

Henry saw him moping and came over to join him. "Its progress, I'm afraid," he said to Cuthbert. "I have been all over the world and it's the same everywhere. Generations of theatre traditions swept away by the cinema. People would walk for days in the past to see a troupe of performing players, Valleys like this would be a natural amphitheatre and the crowds would love it. A market usually sprang up around the event and it was the highlight of the year. Now they have a choice of four or five films several times a night, it's warm, it's comfortable and there is a car park."

Patting Cuthbert sympathetically on the shoulder, he went back to his role as 'Mine host'.

A chair scraped on the other side of the table and a pair of turned-down wellies came into view. Percy sat down and studied his friend. "So what's the story behind Aunt Liza, then?" he asked.

Cuthbert mentally wound back the years, shivered and began to tell him.

"Mum's sister was never interested in the family. She was a rich aunt who had the knack of arriving at embarrassing moments and tutting a lot. She had a daughter, Liza. I was supposed to entertain this Liza whenever they visited. She was one of that type of girl who was always whispering to her mother, but if you challenged her, all you got was, 'Speak up, Cuthbert. If it's not fit to say, then it's not fit to be heard'. This Liza would stand there simpering with her red ringlets and soppy clothes, and get away with everything. I won a box of jelly-babies at a raffle one time and, sure enough, they came to visit that same night. Liza insisted on cutting all the feet off the jelly-babies to play hospitals with them, and all the nice flavoured ones kept disappearing. When I asked her about them, she said they had died and gone to jelly-heaven. So I hid and watched, and as soon as she put a red one to her lips, I jumped out and caught her. She flounced off crying and told the adults she was only kissing it better, and I was sent to bed."

Cuthbert stared morosely at the table top. "Don't underestimate her, Percy. She is the original red devil."

Percy tipped his hat back on his head and contributed, "My mum always said that jelly-babies were Leprechauns caught sticking an extra leaf to clover so they could sell them to tourists as good luck charms."

Cuthbert, deep in his own pool of self-pity, was not thinking straight at that moment, but a moment later he wished he had been. "I didn't know you were Irish," he blurted, before he could stop himself.

Percy shuffled to make himself more comfortable and said, "Not technically, but one of the family was competing in a bowls match and hitched a lift on the Spanish Armada."

Cuthbert gaped and Percy exploited the gap in credibility to continue. "The local priest had seen him practising, and for some reason seemed keen to send him abroad. So, he told my ancestor about the people of Spain who were obsessed with balls. There was even an initiation which involved 'running with the balls', and he paid for his passage."

A crowd had gathered around the table now and Percy gratefully accepted a free pint.

"Anyway, when he got there, it seems there was some misunderstanding. The Spaniards were not interested in balls, it was bulls. Now, my ancestor was at a bit of a loss, so he took a job as a street cleaner in a town called Pamplona and he always kept a bowling ball in his cart to practise if he found a straight and empty street. This particular day, some fool left a gate open just where he had been sweeping and all the bulls started to form up ready to escape. A warning was shouted in Spanish and of course it meant nothing to him - all he knew was that a straight street had emptied right in front of him. So, pulling out his ball, he took aim down the street and let fly just as a herd of bulls thundered around the corner. The ball skittled the legs out from under the first bull. The bull slid sideways, causing the next bull to tumble over him, digging his horns into the ground and stopping dead just as the rest cannoned into them from behind. Apparently the Mayor and his family had been coming up the street the other way and he saved their lives. He was given a medal and passage home, and the event is still celebrated to this day when the people of Pamplona 'run with the bulls'."

Percy sat back until some fool asked, "And the Armada?"

Cuthbert groaned and Percy sat up again.

"Well," he said, "all these ships were heading for England and with a Spanish medal around his neck he had no trouble getting a lift. Of course, he needed to practise because he was playing against the Navy when he got home. As soon as it got dark, he would use Spanish cannonballs to preserve his 'lucky ball' for the big match. With the ships pitching about, this wasn't easy. One of the cannonballs flew over the scuppers and hit the hull of the galleon on his left. They thought they were under attack and turned for home. The next one flew straight down the deck, up the poop deck ladder, and crashed through the stern windows of the flagship, Santissima Trinidad in front of them. This was the Admiral's cabin and he ordered full sail to escape. This left everyone else trailing behind, and after a few more practice bowls, several of them were a good bit lower in the water than when they had started out.

When the dawn came, the Armada was spread out in an ungainly pattern and the Lizard Point was in sight. My ancestor saw his chance and sent a signal to the shore, 'Don't start without me, Drakey, be with you around noon'.

This is why Francis Drake was in no hurry. He thought he had a spy on board, so he finished his game. Anyway, between the battles and the storms, my ancestor ended up being shipwrecked on the coast of Ireland and that's where we heard about the Leprechauns."

Chapter Twelve

Cuthbert stayed on at the pub. He sat alone in his corner wondering why things couldn't stay as they had been.

The Valley had not changed since the Romans detoured around it, yet now, nothing was the same as it had been the last week. He sighed, and placing his empty glass on the bar, he began to saunter home.

The new beige-coloured roads were certainly easy to follow, thought Cuthbert as he stepped out of the way of a large van coming towards him. The van roared past with a whirr of tyres and a strange, familiar 'bonging' sound was heard.

Cuthbert continued on his way but hesitated when he spotted Percy sat on the stile looking troubled.

By the side of him was the crow whose dejection would have looked more convincing if he had known what the problem was.

Cuthbert wandered over to them and perched on the dry-stone wall. No-one said anything and it became a wall of silence.

Whatever Percy had told the crow, it must have been devastating; the bird spread its wings half way out for balance and walked with great melancholy along the top of the wall until it simply dropped off the end.

"Something wrong?" asked Cuthbert.

Percy nodded gloomily and watched his wellies flap as he swung his little legs.

"Well, what is it?" Cuthbert demanded.

"Not going in the house, are you?" mumbled Percy.

Cuthbert pushed himself off the wall and said, "I certainly am. I am ready to jump into bed."

"Not from here, you're not," mumbled Percy.

Cuthbert stopped. "What are you on about, Percy? And stop mumbling."

Percy mumbled away to himself as Cuthbert went into the house. He was still mumbling when Cuthbert ran screaming across the farmyard. "Burglars, thieves, nobody leave the room."

Cuthbert ran around in a demented spiral until he reached his boundaries and started to spiral back in again. He stood doubled up and out of breath in front of Percy who mumbled, "I tried to tell you."

"Was that my clock on the van?" gasped Cuthbert.

"Yep," said Percy.

"Was my bed on that van?" he gasped again.

"Yep," replied Percy.

"Was my ... ?"

Percy interrupted him. "It was all on the van," he said. "Aunt Liza called an auction house in and shifted the lot."

Cuthbert ran out of steam and slumped against the wall.

Percy volunteered, "She said it was time for a clear-out of all the old useless items, and that if I didn't shut up, I would be next."

Cuthbert was appalled. Everything had gone: all his inherited furniture, the family portraits and even the actors' wardrobe from the theatre. This meant effectively that Cuthbert's wardrobe had gone too.

Cuthbert looked at Percy and asked, "When is the sale?"

"Tomorrow," muttered Percy.

* * *

The local saleroom was packed. The front row was made up of sightseers with flasks and sandwiches. The next rows were used by the sightseers too mean to buy sandwiches, and the only real buyers were stood along the back.

The auctioneer climbed up into an old church pulpit, savouring the novel sensation of being taller that everyone else. He announced, "We will start the sale with the property of a gentleman."

Cuthbert's back stiffened in spite of himself and he felt a moment's pride until the auctioneer added, "Three gold watches." He coughed before adding, "Then miscellaneous furniture from some chap in the Valley ... "

"Who is she?" asked Percy.

"Who?" snarled Cuthbert.

"Miss Ellaneous?"

Cuthbert was too busy seething to reply. 'We'll see who's miscellaneous,' he thought. Looking around the room, Cuthbert spotted the antique dealer from the next Valley, Martin Hepplewhite, the man who had tried to buy things from his farm once.

He was the one to watch and Cuthbert drew Percy to one side for a whispered conference.

Martin was quickly making notes in his catalogue and circling lot numbers. He hadn't bought the catalogue; he left that for the amateurs.

The people on the front row always put a catalogue on their seat to reserve it while they viewed the items for sale and Martin simply picked one up. Ticking off another lot smugly, he became aware of a presence in front of him.

Lowering his catalogue slowly revealed first a rather scruffy trilby hat, then a shock of apparently exploded hair surrounding a face from the 'Turnip-carvers catalogue'.

" 'ow do," said Percy. "Not many of us professionals here, then?"

"Er, no," replied Martin as his gaze reached the turned down wellies.

"Good thing," said Percy cheerfully. "Can't have too many peas in a pod, I always say,"

"Do you?" asked Martin, trying desperately to concentrate on what the auction clerk was holding up.

Percy moved away, tapping pieces of furniture and shaking his head sadly as he contemplated the offerings.

Martin pulled his mind back to the business at hand. There was some excellent stuff here today, and after changing the road signs around in the Valleys and locking a few gates, he was the only dealer here. 'Lord knows who that strange twerp is,' he thought.

The bidding plodded on.

Martin was patient. These rural auctioneers gave as much time to an old tin bath as they did to a Chippendale chair. Looking into his Styrofoam cup, Martin decided to go outside to the caravan and get a fresh cup before the good furniture went under the hammer.

Standing at the drop-down flap and trying to ignore the smell of grease which seemed to crawl out from behind it and permeate everyone's clothing, he clutched his cup and turned.

"Not bought anything yet, then?" asked Percy.

"No, not yet," replied Martin, trying to edge away.

Percy synchronised his steps and Martin simply ended up trapped in a corner. Percy looked around in a conspiratorial manner before tapping his nose. "I expect you've spotted the best lot," he suggested in a whisper.

"Perhaps," said Martin slowly, scenting business.

Percy looked around again and beckoned Martin to follow him. This often happened if you appeared on someone else's patch; money

34

changed hands and one of you went home with a profit and an empty van.

Martin followed Percy and found himself ushered into an outbuilding with a stable door.

"The real surprise is in here," Percy was saying as they both entered. The room was gloomy but it was obvious that it was empty.

"There's nothing here," stated Martin.

"Well, I'll be damned," said Percy and he grasped the door handle, tugging it with all his might. "We're locked in," he gasped, turning purple with effort as he cleverly jammed part of his arm against the opening and pretended it was locked.

Martin sipped at his coffee and regretted it. He usually only bought it to warm his hands. He watched Percy battle valiantly for a while before he bent down, pushed the bottom half of the door open, and poured his hot coffee into a welly as he went out.

Inside the auction room, Cuthbert waited. He was hidden in a corner and he had been very busy indeed. He stood at the centre of an almost invisible cobweb of fishing line. He noticed Martin come back in and Percy looking around frantically for him.

He stayed hidden.

Martin was psyching himself up for the succession of items he wanted, forcing himself to relax. Nervous glances towards the door showed that no other dealers had found their way there yet, and when Percy appeared in front of him again, he simply rested his catalogue on top of his hat.

Very close to the moment now, Martin felt the familiar tension begin. This was the thrill of the find, this was what it was all about, this was ... damned peculiar.

He stared hard at the suit of armour behind the auctioneer. He could have sworn that the visor had lifted and lowered itself again. He looked around - no-one else seemed to have noticed. He shook his head to clear his vision, and concentrated.

A gasp went up from the middle row. He followed their eyes and watched in disbelief as a top drawer began to creep open unaided. He looked back to the front and a coffer lid was opening slowly. The suit of armour was raising one hand as if it was bidding, and the visor was opening and closing as if it was laughing at them all.

The audience sat spellbound.

The auctioneer hesitated as he sensed that things were not as they should be.

The room was hushed.

The spell was broken as the coffer lid slammed down, the knight's arm and visor clanged down, and the large clock began to chime an insane clanging rhythm. Cuthbert yanked hard on one of the lines and a drawer shot out of a mahogany carcass and flew across the room, just as someone shouted, "It's the furniture from Mandrake Hall. It's haunted!"

Another similar voice cried, "Why didn't it burn in the fire?"

Someone screamed, "We're doomed," because someone always says this.

The stampede started. Everyone fled for the exits. Catalogues flew into the air, flasks were abandoned and sandwiches were puréed underfoot in the chaos.

Martin tried hard to understand and to keep his feet under him. He failed on both counts and was trampled in the doorway. When he came to, the auctioneer was shaking hands with that strange undertaker chap from the Valley and all the good furniture was being carried outside.

He staggered outside to see the suit of armour being put into a van. As he watched, the helmet creaked around towards him and the visor seemed to smile.

Martin passed out again.

Walking home from the auction was a way of winding down after all the excitement. Cuthbert swung his arms jauntily and Percy pushed his borrowed wheelbarrow. The trick with all the fishing line had worked a treat. Getting there early had paid off.

Percy was miffed because he hadn't been warned and he had panicked like everyone else. Besides, Cuthbert hadn't even thanked him for all his efforts. When he lost sight of his friend, he had consulted the list and tried to buy back all Cuthbert's stuff. Now he had to push it all home because the vans were full.

The arguing started about then.

"Percy, it said rocking horse, not vaulting horse," insisted Cuthbert.

Percy grumbled alongside him.

"And it was cuckoo clocks, not box of socks."

Percy grumbled some more.

"I can't explain the stuffed gorilla at all, I really can't" added Cuthbert.

Percy mumbled and grumbled.

And what the blazes is that on your head? You look like a storm-trooper. I wonder what happened to the pelmet, Cuthbert mused.

Chapter Thirteen

Back at the farm, Cuthbert and Percy were greeted by site Manager, Anita Peace, overseeing the unloading of the vans from the auctioneers.

Several construction workers were off-loading items into the theatre, of all places.

Cuthbert hurried forward to confront her, and Percy tried to keep up with a wheelbarrow full of junk and a helmet bouncing about on his head like a chamber-pot.

"What do you think you're doing?" asked Cuthbert indignantly.

Anita slowly teased a long blonde piece of stray hair back under the rim of her yellow helmet and replied languidly, "Following orders."

Cuthbert fumed, "Oh, right, that's what they all say."

"All whom?" asked Anita innocently.

Cuthbert spluttered, "All the ones who say they're following orders."

Anita asked, "Ah, lot of it about is there?"

"Lot of what?" demanded Cuthbert.

"A lot of order as the result of following orders," she purred. "In fact, order out of chaos," she reasoned.

Cuthbert's riposte consisted of grunts, gasps and half-formed hand movements, but he noticed that Anita was smiling gently as she looked over his shoulder.

Glancing to one side at Percy, and seeing him trying to slick his hair down, Cuthbert knew exactly who was coming.

He turned. The dust cloud was hanging over the farm gate and heading this way rapidly. Percy stood rigidly to attention and Anita preened.

Aunt Liza zoomed silently towards them and skidded to a halt, peppering them with gravel. She smiled at Anita and announced, "Tried to let you know I was coming but the batteries are flat", and turning to Percy, she rapped her walkie-talkie on his helmet with a resounding 'clang', which caused it to spin round on his head and slowly vibrate him into the ditch.

"What are you doing with my furniture?" demanded Cuthbert.

38

Aunt Liza looked calmly back at him and said, "Our furniture Cuthbert. We're family."

Cuthbert took a deep breath and then he spotted something awful. He pointed at the front of her scooter and, hand shaking, asked, "Is that blind Pugh?"

For one awful moment Cuthbert thought that Aunt Liza had encountered the Valley's blind and deaf sheepdog, and wreaked a terrible revenge.

"Oh, silly boy," laughed Aunt Liza. "It's the head from a toy dog the twins fitted for me. When I reach the speed limit, its ears flap up to warn me." She patted his hand and added, "Don't worry, Blind Pugh and I have an agreement. He leaves me alone and I will unravel his tail from around the back wheel and give it back."

With that, she sped silently into the house with Anita in her wake.

Chapter Fourteen

Cuthbert sat on the edge of the stage with his head on his hands.

Percy was bouncing about on the tractor seat mimicking driving a tank. Cuthbert didn't bother to tell him that tanks don't have steering wheels.

All around him on the stage was his furniture. It looked like a set from 'Sleuth', or it would have done with some old weapons on the walls.

Percy broke into his thoughts with, "Where shall we put all this stuff when the rehearsals start?"

Cuthbert sat bolt upright. The rehearsals - no-one had approached him to vie for the best parts. People had stopped putting an arm around him and steering him into corners for 'A quiet word'. The rot had set in already. No-one wanted to be in his play.

Just then, the two main doors crashed open and the Valley's leading man entered. Quickly striking a pose in silhouette, he strode down the aisle, patting Percy on the shoulder and knocking him clean off his seat on the way.

"There you are sport," he boomed, leaping up onto the stage with a mighty bound just as a stray sunbeam entered and glinted on his teeth. "I need some help, sport," he began.

At least the arm was back around Cuthbert's shoulder and they were weaving in and out of the scattered furniture.

"Went to see one of those new movies on my holidays. I wanted to see what your Aunt Liza was bringing to the Valley." He stopped and looked Cuthbert squarely in the eyes. "I loved it," he said. "I can be seen by millions. The camera can zoom right in so that the dimples shows. Some of the babes in the back row don't get that in here, you know," he confided.

Cuthbert walked, weaved and listened as the milkman's ambition was laid bare. Apparently he had been practising and he could now rappel down a cliff-face, do a forward roll, and come up with two guns blazing and not a hair out of place.

"What do you think, sport?"

He stood before Cuthbert like a muscle-bound Peter Pan, all the innocence and hope of the Valley etched into his features.

Cuthbert sat him down. He explained that they would not be making the films. The films would come from all over the world and all the people of the Valley could do was pay for a ticket and sit and watch them.

When Cuthbert explained gently that the theatre would now close and all the acting was finished, the man visibly deflated, and without another word he dragged his feet back to where he had parked his cart and drove slowly away.

Cuthbert stood amongst his belongings and let the melancholia wash over him. His head hung and the theatre seemed very dark.

A scuffling sound behind him caused him to turn, and he yelped in terror as a huge beast with red eyes appeared to lunge at him with a roar.

Cuthbert ran backwards, falling over his chaise-longue in the process.

Floundering to his feet, Cuthbert found Percy laughing fit to burst and hanging onto his stuffed gorilla for support.

Cuthbert sensed the red mist descending.

Percy hesitated and said, "Just thought you needed a laugh, that's all."

Cuthbert stared. That was it; they wouldn't take this lying down. They would attack, guerrilla warfare style!

Cuthbert ran to an old sword chest and dragged out a large scimitar with a scrape as the blade left the scabbard.

Percy looked on in horror as Cuthbert swung and decapitated the beast, and then slashed it vertically down the back before lopping both hind legs off.

He stood panting.

"Er … " began Percy.

"Get in," replied Cuthbert.

"Pardon?" goggled Percy.

"Get inside. It's a disguise," demanded Cuthbert.

"Why me?" wailed Percy.

"Because I have the sword?" suggested Cuthbert.

It was a rather short gorilla which stood facing Cuthbert. Percy's legs stuck through the holes at the bottom of its trunk and the rest of the fur trailed behind, suggesting that Daddy Bear had mated with a seal at some stage. The red glass eyes had been popped out and Percy's eyes sometimes lined up with the holes depending on what he was doing.

Percy hadn't been all that keen until Cuthbert allowed him to wear his hat on top. Percy thought this would protect him if another gorilla showed up.

Well mistakes do happen.

Chapter Fifteen

The next day, Cuthbert and Percy visited the village and subtly tried to discover who was in favour of the cinema and who was against.

It was time to nail one's colours to the mast.

Percy hadn't noticed a mast in the Valley and he wasn't convinced that Cuthbert knew which colour they should nail to it.

The argument kept them company all the way into the village. They were interrupted in mid-flow by a voice hissing at them over a hedge just at the village boundary.

Cuthbert turned one way and faced someone in a balaclava with a yellow plastic hat on top. Percy faced the other way and faced a cow.

The voice said, "Don't panic, I am on your side."

Now the man had his balaclava on backwards for extra secrecy and Cuthbert could not see his lips moving.

However, Percy could definitely see the cow's lips moving as it chewed the cud.

"Who are you?" asked Cuthbert.

"I am an uninvolved party," said the man, or the cow, depending on where you were standing.

"But you are wearing a construction site hat," observed Cuthbert.

Both the man and the cow fell silent for a while. Eventually, the impasse was broken.

"It's a disguise and a damn good one," said Percy to the cow.

The man with the woolly face leaned forward into the hedge and said, "It's not a supermarket, it's a cinema." A finger appeared over its mouth and he said, "That's all for now, I will keep you abreast," and he scuttled off under cover of the hedge.

"That's really good of you," said Percy to the cow. "I like a nice bit of chicken."

The rest of the walk was in silence, each with his own thoughts, and they definitely weren't compatible.

Chapter Sixteen

The Mandrake Arms was quiet. Henry was cleaning glasses and pleased to have even their company.

Cuthbert told him about the strange encounter and Henry nodded wisely.

Percy jumped up and down. "Now me," he said. "My encounter now."

Cuthbert glared and said, "It was the same encounter, you twit."

Percy sulked on his stool and listened. It didn't sound the same to him at all.

Henry leaned on the bar. "You've got a deep throat," he said knowledgeably.

"Well, thank you very much" said Cuthbert nervously, displaying a puzzled expression. He had heard about strange men in bars.

"No, you fool," snarled Henry. "It's a term for an informer. The Americans had a case involving someone high up in the Government and this chap appeared in the dark in underground car parks and gave them vital information." He paused. "He would only identify himself as Deep Throat."

"Oh," said a relieved Cuthbert.

"Looked like a Freisian to me," muttered Percy.

Cuthbert thought about it and said, "He's not going to be much use if he only tells when something's happened, is he?"

Henry shrugged.

Percy muttered, "You spend your life leaning on a hedge and see if you can do any better."

"What?" asked Cuthbert.

"Getting cold, need a sweater," chirped Percy brightly.

It was soon obvious that the business people would not be behind them. A cinema would bring lots of custom to the Valley, Henry explained.

Parking fees from some muddy old field, a swift pint and a Cornish pasty on the way home. Even Mrs. Biggle at the Post Office stood to profit. Margery, of course, was married to Henry now and running the Mandrake Arms, so she would share in the windfall.

The milkman might even put extra deliveries before acting when it came to the crunch. The Captain and his wife Elspeth were a possibility - they had retired and both loved the theatre.

Belinda, the barmaid, would probably get paid extra, so she was out. It was going to be up to the real Valley folk to be the guerrilla force, plus Percy of course. He had the suit.

Chapter Seventeen

The meeting took place at the old mill to take advantage of the tunnel system which undermined the Valley. Some of the tunnels had been to channel water to the mill and others were just for general sneaking about.

The Captain cleared his throat and began with a roll-call. "Myself, of course, my dear wife … "

Elspeth nodded to the assembly like the dormouse at the Mad Hatter's tea party.

"Cuthbert, Percy, the twins and Whistle," the Captain continued.

'Whistle' had appeared on the night of the meeting without a word. No-one had seen him in months and he just sat at the table, face completely hidden by his hood.

Elspeth had clucked around him, and several sandwiches and a cup of tea had disappeared into the hood, but no words had come out.

"Cuthbert, would you like to start?" barked the Captain, fully in charge of those around his campaign table.

Cuthbert stood and surveyed those around the table. "We all know who the enemy is," he stated dramatically. "The enemy is anyone involved in the construction of the cinema. In fact, we need to set up twenty-four hour surveillance on Aunt Liza so that we are not discovered."

Cuthbert paused, rather pleased with himself.

"No need, it's already done," murmured one of the twins looking at a screen on his lap.

"What do you mean?" asked the Captain.

The other twin glanced onto his brother's lap and said, "She's just returning to the farmhouse as we speak."

Everyone clustered around behind the twin and peered over his shoulder. Sure enough, the farmhouse was seen approaching at speed, a door flew open and the view was of Cuthbert's kitchen.

"The dog's head," gasped Cuthbert in admiration. "Well done, boys." He resisted the temptation to pat them on the head. Old lessons die hard.

The door crashed open and a figure was framed against the night sky. "Good evening, gentlemen," it hissed.

Elspeth was about to speak when she recognised Ronald, and stayed quiet.

Ronald slammed the door and threw a yellow plastic hat and a balaclava onto the table. "Someone wearing these popped up from behind a wall, so I garrotted him," he announced

"Did you kill him?" asked an alarmed Captain.

"No, I just got all his vital information and let him go," said Ronald smugly. "He won't be back."

"He'd better be," gasped Percy. "He's Mister Deep Throat from America."

Ronald looked around in disgust. "He would have been 'Mister Squeaky' if the wall hadn't been there."

Walking around the table he checked the view from the camera fitted by the twins. "Excellent," he said. "We need men like you to compensate for men like these." He swept an arm around the room and laughed at his own quip as the twins finished picking his pockets.

A variety of knives, clubs and knuckle-dusters were distributed under the table and everyone fantasised about using them on Ronald.

"Now," began Ronald, "thanks to me we now know the whole plan ... " He paused dramatically and wondered why no-one reacted. Jealous, he thought. "It isn't a supermarket at all." He waited, as everyone finished cleaning their fingernails with his knives and said importantly, "It's a c ... "

"CINEMA," chorused everyone loudly.

"Oh!" said Ronald.

The meeting had gradually become a pointless squabble about spheres of influence and structures of command, and all the little cakes had gone anyway, so they all began to make their way home.

Cuthbert and Percy used the tunnel and the echoing footsteps kept them company. Neither of them had much to say, and when they both thought of something and stopped to talk, the footsteps didn't.

They both ran like the wind. In fact, they ran so fast that they went straight past Cuthbert's cellar and found themselves in the reservoir at the top of the hill. Bursting through the rotten planks covering the top, they paused for breath and found themselves face to face with a hooded figure.

"Whistle," breathed Cuthbert in relief, "you won't catch anything at this time of night." He began to giggle hysterically.

"Whistle, see," replied Whistle. "You two frightening the fish certainly won't help."

Percy checked his wellies. They were dry. Shame, walking on water would have looked good on his C.V..

Cuthbert and Percy stood together on the hilltop and stared at the construction site. It lay below them in a blaze of lights from tall towers positioned around a perimeter fence. Huge yellow excavators stood like sleeping dinosaurs, arms and buckets resting wearily on the ground.

Percy sighed. "My Dad spent some time in one of them," he said sadly, "Never the same when he came home."

"Why? Didn't he like building?" asked Cuthbert cautiously.

Percy looked annoyed and snapped, "He was in a prison camp."

Cuthbert was abashed but still suspicious, "Sorry, Percy," he said.

Percy brightened slightly and continued. "He was on the escape committee. He was in charge of all the master plans for great escapes." Percy beamed at the memory.

"Did he?" asked Cuthbert.

"Did he what?" queried Percy.

"Did he escape?" asked Cuthbert.

"'Course not," protested Percy. "How would he run a committee if he escaped?"

Things were silent for a while but Cuthbert knew it was too good to last.

"I remember one story he told me," said Percy, shuffling his wellies to get comfortable.

Cuthbert sighed and sat on a log, only to find that Whistle had joined them and was sat there too.

Cuthbert nodded to Whistle and the hood nodded back.

Just as Percy was taking a deep breath to begin, Cuthbert stopped him.

"How did your Dad get captured?"

Percy hesitated. "Ah well, it was all a bit of a misunderstanding," he began.

Cuthbert smiled. This was more like it - catch Percy by surprise and you may even learn something.

Percy sat down and began. "Dad was in charge of painting those roundels under the aeroplane wings so that you knew whose side the plane was on when it flew over. Well, Dad had an idea. He stayed up all one night and painted black crosses under the wings of all the bombers. He figured out that when they flew over enemy territory, no-one would shoot at them because they were friendly aircraft when seen from below. As soon as he had finished painting them all, he went looking for the Squadron Leader to tell him what he had done.

Unfortunately, the Squadron Commander and all the officers had gone to meet the King and all the top nobs of the Air Force who were visiting later that day to watch the Squadron return home from a mission.

The planes took off and completed the mission. No-one even fired at them. Dad was in the control tower listening to the transmissions as they turned for home and the King and all the top-brass were delighted. Not one plane lost. Just as the King was watching too, Dad approached the Station Commander, saluted, and explained what he had done just as the guns opened fire at the edge of the airfield.

When he turned around, he joined the King and everyone else watching the airfield guns shooting down their own aeroplanes. By the time the last one had crashed, Dad had hidden in the King's plane just to be safe, but he was spotted and they dropped him into a haystack somewhere in France. They thought he would be more use over there, apparently."

No-one said a thing.

Percy cleared his throat and said, "Now, where was I on the great escape story? Oh yes, this particular day the guards allowed them to have a kite-flying competition."

Cuthbert couldn't hold himself back. "They hung onto the ropes and flew over the fence?"

Percy glared. "No," he snapped. "At the same time, they allowed a pole-vaulting competition."

Cuthbert was there again. "They all vaulted over the fence?"

"No," snapped Percy again. "In another part of the camp they were allowed to send messages home on gas-filled balloons."

Cuthbert had it this time. "And they floated over the fence on the balloons?"

"No," snapped Percy for the third time. "In the middle of the camp they were allowed to jump over a vaulting horse and ... "

Cuthbert was there again. "They used it to hide a tunnel and everyone crawled out?"

Percy scoffed. "Don't be ridiculous."

Cuthbert gave up. "Well how many escaped?"

"None," replied Percy smugly.

"None?" gasped Cuthbert. "What was the point of that?"

"That was the clever part. Dad worked it out that if they kept the enemy on edge for the right amount of months, they would take them completely by surprise and walk out of the gates altogether, and that's what they did - they all walked out together."

Cuthbert was impressed. "What did the guards do?" he asked, completely enthralled.

Percy considered him for a moment and said, "Oh, they had all gone. The war ended the day before."

Chapter Eighteen

The twins had a problem.

They had realised early on that this boarding school business could be an earner but back in the Valley others had moved in and taken over the running of things.

The 'Valley-Mafia' was in new hands and their turf would need to be re-taken before this cinema opportunity could be exploited. As natural leaders themselves, it should not be a huge problem, but involving grown-ups was risky, especially the twerps available at short notice.

Ronald was a simple blunt instrument but a good source of weaponry. Cuthbert was always handy if they needed digging tools and had a body to shift.

Mum was busy with the Mandrake Arms and her new husband, so supervision was never a problem. The Captain was quite useful when he showed them his books on tactics, and he still had a field manual for the old cannon, and Elspeth made a cracking scone.

That left Percy. Percy was a real enigma. After a brainstorming session, the twins had thrown about their ideas for his usefulness. One twin came up with 'draught excluder' and the other with 'distraction' - he was being used in that role right now.

After a top-level secret meeting, Percy had been dispatched to find out who was running things. It had to be someone expendable, after all.

Percy sidled up to the litter bin on the playground, hat pulled down and a cigarette in the corner of his mouth. It wasn't lit and it was stuck to his top lip, but if you were doing the job, you had to look the part.

When the twins had run the Valley, the litter bin was fitted with a speaker and all messages were left there, and any new instructions issued.

Percy leaned against it nonchalantly and hissed, "It's me. Are you there?" He scanned the exclusion zone around the bin. Two lads had appeared and sat on the swings watching him. Another two appeared by the gate and bicycle outriders could be seen on the perimeter.

Percy jumped as a voice asked, "Who are you?"

Without turning, Percy hissed, "This is business. I need to see the Head Boy."

He jumped again as a voice at his elbow demanded, "Who told you about the Head Boy?"

Percy had actually been a bit facetious with that one, but he obviously had a feel of this game and he felt quite smug about it.

"Some of us know things," he said, tapping the side of his nose.

The hand movement was a bad idea and Percy slowly lowered it again as small people either side of him tensed and kept up the pressure on the catapult elastic. The sun glinted on ball bearings held in leather pouches and beads of sweat built up on foreheads as the tension mounted.

The boys from the swings were closer now. The outriders had moved in.

A face appeared before Percy. "What do you want?"

The owner of the voice was trying desperately to appear threatening, but the acne and the marker pen side-burns weren't helping.

Percy assumed his role. "What's the word on the street, lads?"

"What street?" came the reply.

"Er ... field? Er ... playground?" tried Percy.

After a nod from the boy in front, the two boys flanking Percy relaxed and retreated a step. Still watchful, and with primary pressure taken up in their elastic, the one in front looked Percy up and down with distaste, and said, "I don't really want to go through your pockets, so what are you going to give us?"

The others had closed in silently and Percy was feeling rather unsure of himself. "Er ... what do you want?"

"Gold, jewels, computer games, girlie magazines ... " The replies were coming from all directions as each one added to the wish list.

Percy rummaged for a moment and asked hopefully, "Ball of string and a Werthers Original?"

An air of menace descended. The one in front growled, "Watch it Mister, there's a lot of concrete being poured in this Valley these days."

Percy began to sweat. Somehow none of the moves taught by the legendary 'Tsun-shine' seemed applicable here, and if you had a memory like Percy's, you were in real trouble anyway.

"Are you going to light that?"

Percy realised that he had forgotten about the limp cigarette dangling from his lip and he nodded mutely. A hand appeared from inside the litter bin and a flame shot out from a lighter.

Percy leaned over and sucked in.

Never having smoked in his life, Percy didn't know what to expect, so when his lungs filled, his eyes burned, and everything coughed from his boots upwards, he panicked. Tearing the offending paper tube from his lip, he automatically threw it into the bin and flailed his arms about to clear the smoke.

Voices yelled, elastic twanged, and ball bearings ricocheted from bikes and park equipment. The plastic litter bin went up with a 'Whooomf', and ran away as fast as its little legs could carry it.

Percy was alone.

The twins collapsed into each other's arms behind the bush, tears running down their faces.

So this was the new 'Valley-Mafia'. They couldn't even wire up a speaker in a litter bin.

Chapter Nineteen

On the construction site, things were progressing nicely. Steel ribs had been built to support the main structure and the excavators fussed around it like carnivores cleaning a carcass.

Aunt Liza sat on her scooter with Anita standing beside her. Both women's hair stirred in the breeze as they watched the work progress. Liza's hair shone like spun copper in the sun and Anita's gleamed like flax.

They represented two very beautiful women with ugly ambitions. The large pannier on the back of the scooter hung open revealing compartments for glasses and a cocktail shaker. The two women chinked their glasses together as they toasted 'success'.

"Can anything disrupt the building work?" Liza asked Anita, turning her head slightly to allow the breeze to sweep away a strand of hair from her face.

Anita watched the activity below and replied, "I don't think so, but I have never seen such odd characters all in one place before. Do you think they will all team up?"

Liza laughed. "If this bunch team up, we will have a three-ring circus to sell tickets for as well as the cinema!"

They both laughed and the glasses chinked again.

Liza continued. "As long as the local businesses think we are good for trade, it will keep them divided. The shopping mall will appear later, when we are established."

Another chink of glass hid the rustle from a nearby bush as a woolly head in a plastic yellow hat slid backwards out of view.

Chapter Twenty

At this evening's meeting, Percy was centre stage. His tales of derring-do eclipsed anything that anyone else had to offer until the twins showed a film of the whole thing projected onto the wall of the Captain's kitchen.

After that, he fell silent.

The twins outlined the need to recruit the Valley-Mafia and bring it back under their control. This would take up most of their time.

The Captain was engaged in a full reconnaissance of the construction site as well as preparing campaign maps.

Elspeth was making cups of tea heavy enough to hold down the corners of the maps.

Ronald was in the process of having a container of surprises delivered by mysterious means from a mysterious source, using a mysterious process. All a bit of a mystery really.

Percy's career as a Deep Throat had been relegated to a 'little squeak' category and put on hold.

Cuthbert sat very quiet and quite pale. The twins had allocated him his role. He was to spy on Aunt Liza and look for clues. He could almost see the shadow of the noose.

A creak from the window made everyone spin around. A woolly face appeared, topped off with a yellow helmet. It looked around, or at least the hat moved from side to side.

Elspeth fainted clean away and Cuthbert announced, "This is Deep Throat, gentlemen."

The hat bobbed up and down in agreement. The visitor tried to speak but all he could produce was a series of wheezes and grunts.

"What is it, man?" snapped the Captain. "Not much of an informer if you don't speak the language."

The vision at the window mimicked being strangled and shaken until his hat nearly fell off, and pointed an accusing finger at Ronald.

Everyone turned but Ronald was completely unconcerned. He had carved his name into the table and was just adding the full stop. "Well, the idiot only told us what we already knew," he snarled.

The man in the window waved his arms frantically to attract their attention back to him, and began a series of elaborate mimes. He mimed Aunt Liza holding onto her handle bars and leaned forward to suggest speed. Then he stood tall, stuck out his chest and mimicked flicking his hair away from his face.

"He's going to buy a motorbike so he can attract the crumpet," suggested Percy, always the first with useful suggestions.

"He felt sick earlier but he's ok now?" tried Cuthbert.

"No, no," said Elspeth from a sitting position on the floor. "He's showing Liza and that Anita together."

A frantic thumbs-up from the window cleared act one and they all waited for act two to begin.

Deep Throat pointed at Cuthbert and Percy, and mimicked juggling, indicating a pointy hat on each of them.

Cuthbert sat up straight and declared smugly, "She is obviously impressed with the way I juggle all my responsibilities and thinks I do a wizard job."

He sat back, content with his analysis.

Elspeth was studying the man carefully. "No, sorry I get 'pair of clowns'," she shrugged apologetically.

The thumbs came up again and Cuthbert slumped lower. Pointing at Ronald, Deep Throat rightly interpreted the look he got in return and moved on. After holding up one finger, he mimicked a large square and a man winding a handle near to his face.

"First the cinema," intoned Elspeth.

Up came the thumbs. After holding up two fingers, he then mimicked someone taking things off a shelf and putting them in a shopping trolley.

"Then the pickpockets," said Ronald. "That's obvious, that is. Where there is a crowd, there's a profit."

The man flapped his hands and the hat pointed towards Elspeth in desperation.

"Scrumpers!" shouted Percy startling everyone. "Someone's going to pinch all the apples."

The hands flapped again.

"Pickpockets," rumbled Ronald.

"Scrumpers," shouted Percy.

Deep Throat stuck two fingers up again and Ronald growled, "Watch it, mate."

Elspeth spoke very quietly but with great conviction. "First the cinema, second the supermarket."

Deep Throat bowed to her and disappeared.

The Captain broke the silence. "That will put everybody out of business. The whole Valley would have to shop there."

Cuthbert would be the only one not affected but he wasn't going to gain any friends by saying it, so he sat quietly.

Percy had been brooding for a while and now he spoke. "Barbed wire," he announced.

"Where?" asked Ronald. "Around the building site?"

"No," replied Percy in exasperation. "Around the apple trees."

Chapter Twenty-One

Percy bounced along inside the tunnel as they made their way home, but Cuthbert dragged his feet and trailed behind.

'Spying on Aunt Liza? Couldn't he do something easy like wrestle the earthmovers to a standstill, or emigrate?' he thought.

Percy stood waiting for him, head cocked on one side like an inquisitive puppy. He had cheered up once everyone made it clear that the apples were safe. In fact, no-one in the room could think where there were any apples.

"You are not scared of Aunt Liza, are you?" asked Percy, relishing the moment.

Cuthbert's first impulse was to lie and come over all macho, but he didn't do macho very well. "Percy," he said, "I have been terrified of that little tattle-tale since the day I first laid eyes on her. In fact I was in trouble several seconds after first laying eyes on her."

Cuthbert idly kicked at a pebble and it clattered down the tunnel. A few seconds later, it clattered back towards them.

The cellar entrance was only yards away and they both went for it. Anybody watching all those arms and legs flailing about stuck in that little hole would have thought Medusa was making a house call.

And there was a watcher!

The pair burst into Cuthbert's kitchen from the cellar steps, still tangled together as they tumbled towards the stairs.

"Oh boys, you just can't wait, can you?" Aunt Liza smirked as she glided away to her ground floor bedroom at the end of the house. The two of them glared at her as she disappeared, dusted themselves down and sat on the bottom step.

Percy looked thoughtful and said, "What does she keep in all those bags?"

"Which bags?" enquired Cuthbert gloomily.

"The ones she keeps on the back of the scooter," said Percy.

"I thought she only had one."

"No, there's a roomful of them between here and her bedroom." Percy was definite. "I fell over one in the dark, and when I turned around I fell over another one."

Cuthbert looked at him keenly. "What were you doing in there in the dark, Percy?"

Percy gave a sheepish shuffle, recognised by all guilty sheep everywhere, and replied, "Well, I thought that the chap with the woolly face and the hat looked pretty good, so I tried for tights and a trilby as my persona non grata, but I couldn't find any."

Cuthbert decided to drop that line of enquiry and follow the original. "Where are these bags?" he asked.

"Just through there," said Percy, nodding to the door Aunt Liza had just gone through. "There's a room there, just before her bedroom."

Cuthbert glared and said, "I know. It's my house."

After several cups of tea to let the house settle down, and for Liza to be deeply asleep, Cuthbert stood up. "Its time," he announced.

Leaving Percy at the table, he went towards the door to the other room. Opening it with the skill of a house-owner who knows every quirk of his property, he stepped inside.

As Cuthbert's eyes adjusted to the gloom, he used the moonlight from the window to find his way about. Liza had transferred to another, smaller scooter to go through the old doorways and the monster she usually rode sat watching him with one baleful eye blinking at him.

After a moment's panic, Cuthbert realised that it was simply re-charging from the power-point.

Marvellous, he thought. Electricity was a novelty in the Valley. It was so irregular that kettles were still boiled over fires and yet Liza managed to charge up every night. Then he spotted the cable running through the open window. The crafty devil had coupled it up to a generator on the construction site.

Moving slowly around, Cuthbert sensed that he was being watched. As he moved nearer to the scooter, he heard a faint whirring sound. One of the dog's eyes was following him.

Moving right up to the lens, he whispered, "Shouldn't you two be asleep?"

The lens whirred to the left and then to the right. Cuthbert went over to one of the big rectangular cases which fitted to the back of the scooter. Percy was right, there were several of them.

The first one he unzipped had compartments for glasses and some kind of flask with a jar of olives at the bottom. The next one was heavy; there was a spare hammer drill and all its accessories.

59

The next one had spanners, all graded and fastened in rows - it was a mobile workshop. The next one was unzipped and it revealed a concertina system of compartments full of maps, all with coded markings at strategic points.

Cuthbert slipped a couple of them into his pocket and tried another case. His heart almost stopped - it was full of handguns, all shapes and sizes, and some had silencers on. The bottom part was filled with boxes of ammunition. He hastily zipped it up and retreated.

Chapter Twenty-Two

Percy was waiting for him, and Cuthbert pulled him outside without either speaking. They were well clear of the house when Cuthbert slowed to a walk and told Percy what he had seen.

Together they headed for the Mandrake Arms. Henry was just the man to show this evidence to.

The bar was open and the Captain and Elspeth were inside. Margery served them both with hot chocolate and they all sat at a large table. Cuthbert spread out his map and everyone leaned forward. At some point the twins' heads appeared amongst the crowd and nobody noticed.

"There," Cuthbert announced. "What did I tell you all?"

Everyone peered at the lines of curving streets and the coded symbols scattered about on each side of the roads.

"What is it?" asked the Captain.

"Isn't it obvious?" squealed Cuthbert

"No," replied the whole group. Everyone peered closely and Margery suddenly said, "Just a minute, I think I see a pattern." She concentrated for a moment and smiled "Oh I like this woman," she said admiringly.

"Well, what is it?" cried the group simultaneously.

Letting the tension build, Margery put one beautifully manicured nail onto the first symbol. "That's Dorothy Pumpkins."

The nail moved, "That's 'Last', and that one is 'Marks and Sparks'." The nail slid along the network of streets naming every dress shop, shoe shop and female hide-away in the nearest city. The moving finger wrote and having writ pointed at Cuthbert as everyone collapsed laughing at him.

Cuthbert felt his ears redden, and when the hysteria died down, he slapped down another map. "How about that one, then?"

His audience gasped.

Cuthbert was vindicated, but it brought no pleasure to the assembly. In the silence, imaginations were working overtime.

Shops and pubs were closing for the last time. People who kept their independence by owning a business and running their own lives

61

might actually have to work for someone else. Good grief - shelf stacking!

The new map showed the Valley, but not the Valley anyone around this table recognised. It was dominated by a gigantic cinema complex which was joined onto an equally gigantic supermarket which had spawned a gigantic shopping mall.

From above, the deviousness was revealed. All the roads which had been levelled for Aunt Liza's 'easy access', only needed the odd house knocked down and they would all join up. She had already laid the foundations.

"Oh Lord," whispered Henry, "it's another Silicone Valley."

Margery briefly considered implants and Percy perked up. "Is that where they make plastic flowers?" he asked, seeing a job opportunity.

It was a miserable crowd making its way home that night, but at least 'the resistance' had gained new members.

As Henry had pointed out, "Adversity makes the best recruiting posters."

Cuthbert chimed in with, "The devil has all the best tunes."

Percy contributed, "Grandma makes the thickest socks."

* * *

Percy and Cuthbert sat on the old stone wall by the stile, lost in their own thoughts. The crow hopped closer and tried to analyse Percy's jacket before he pecked it, but decided that some things were even worse than carrion.

Percy broke the silence of the night. "Why is she in that thing anyway?"

Cuthbert roused himself. "Who, in what and where?" he asked.

Percy clarified the question. "Aunt Liza, why is she on that scooter?"

Cuthbert thought for a long moment and replied. "So that she can catch everyone else, I think".

The silence descended once more. The crow was feeling uneasy. It wasn't the company; he was used to these two.

No, the feathers were standing up on the back of his neck and he slowly turned. He met the eyes of a large rat but not the bright, inquisitive eyes normally associated with rattus rattus - this one was dead.

It was also several feet above the ground and strapped to a boy's head. The Valley-Mafia's surveillance system was getting sloppy.

Chapter Twenty-Three

Neither Cuthbert nor Percy was in any hurry to enter the farmhouse. Sleep didn't seem a good idea in the Valley anymore. When you awoke, the building you fell asleep in could have become something else entirely different.

"Percy?" Cuthbert wasn't sure where this question was coming from and he knew he was asking for trouble, but he asked it anyway. "How did you get into gardening?"

Percy gave Cuthbert a suspicious look, thought for a moment and said, "That's easy. My uncle kept chickens on an allotment and I would sneak up there and offer to help. Apparently, they had a part-time job testing beer, so when I was there, they could concentrate on that job while I kept an eye on the chickens." Percy shuffled, trying to find comfort on a stone wall and continued. "One day, I heard my uncle ask Dad whether I was taking care of the chickens or the chickens were taking care of me. He reckoned it was a toss-up which of us was actually in charge. Well, I took this as a challenge and pinched one of Mum's red washing-up gloves and put it on top of my head to look like a rooster."

Cuthbert began to pay attention as the image presented itself to a mind supposedly immune to 'Percyisms' by now.

"After sitting in the middle of the chicken run with them for a bit, they accepted me as one of their own and I started an experiment. For some reason, one of the real roosters kept trying to climb onto one of the chickens and had to flap his wings like mad to stay there. Well, the next day I took a load of rubber bands with me and started fastening chickens' feet to chickens' backs until I had a pyramid. Then, I found that if the top one flapped its wings, they would all move forward together. I had invented the first chicken circus."

Cuthbert's mind went to that place the mystics strive so hard to find. It was the only defence against Percy.

Percy continued as the memories came flooding back, "That was only the beginning; I found a bicycle designed for Action Man and taught one of them to ride it. Then, as it learnt to pedal faster, it started jumping through a flaming hoop. One of the others could hold its breath for ages after I trained it with rubber-bands around its beak and it would dive into the rain butt and sit on the bottom." Percy sighed, "It took months you know, but it was worth it. I was determined to show my uncle that I wasn't as dumb as a chicken."

Cuthbert was completely in the grip of this one. "Well, what happened?" he demanded.

Percy seemed to deflate, his shoulders slumped. "Dad and my uncle had been testing beer all day in the allotment shed and I had this extravaganza planned for when they came out. I discovered that if I put colouring in the chicken feed they would leave a coloured trail behind them when they flew, just like the Red Arrows.

They had clipped wings, so they could only fly from the fence posts on one side to posts on the other side. A side-effect was that the feathers turned the same colour as the vapour trail. Anyway, this day there was a visitor in the shed, the gamekeeper from the nature reserve.

He came out first with a shotgun over his shoulder. I clapped and the extravaganza began. The gamekeeper staggered out from a long testing session to find himself being buzzed by coloured chickens leaving smoke trails, and when he turned to watch them, he saw an advancing pyramid of chickens lurching towards him. Just at that moment, from the opposite direction, a chicken on a bicycle flew past with its feathers on fire."

Percy slumped even lower as he was forced to reveal the inevitable.

"He naturally assumed it was an attack of 'the blue-devils', opened fire and cleared the whole display with two well aimed bursts of buck-shot."

Percy paused and added mournfully, "When Dad and my uncle came out from behind it, all they saw was me with a red rubber glove on my head and a yard full of feathers. My uncle nudged Dad and said, 'What did I tell you? Daft as a brush', and they walked away."

Chapter Twenty-Four

Walking to the evening meeting, Cuthbert managed to ask Percy, "How did the 'chicken circus' introduce you to gardening?"

Percy replied, "Well, it meant that I spent hours up on the allotments. Some of the men really did go up there to do some gardening and I used to watch them. Why?"

Cuthbert shrugged. "I just thought that I might learn some of your secrets," he said lightly.

Percy stopped dead, appalled. "Do you know what I had to go through to learn those secrets?" He was staring hard at Cuthbert now. "Is that why you're always hanging around? I had to go through the 'seven levels' before I could be initiated." He shuddered at the memory and put his hands on his hips. "Nothing would prise those secrets from me. I took the oath."

Cuthbert walked on, saying dismissively, "I was only showing interest. What can be so secret about 'Dig a hole, plant a seed and stand and watch?'," he enquired sarcastically.

Percy was aghast. "How do you know the first three levels?"

Cuthbert shook his head and walked on.

Percy was demanding, "How come you are always there, eh? How come I see you every day and every meal time, eh? Answer me that."

Cuthbert sighed and looked him straight in the eye. "Percy, you live in my house."

"Oh," said Percy.

Chapter Twenty-Five

The atmosphere in the mill kitchen was tense. As Cuthbert took his place, he noticed another balaclava and yellow plastic helmet on the table. 'Oh no, not again,' he thought.

Ronald was watching him. "What do you think?" he asked proudly.

Cuthbert replied, "I think he's going to run out of balaclavas soon."

Ronald snorted and said, "That's not all," and with a flourish he slid a large dead rat across the table as if he were raising the stakes in a poker game.

A shudder ran around the table. Cuthbert ran an expert eye over the rodent. "It's dead," he announced.

Ronald exploded. "Of course its dead. It attacked me." He thumped the table for emphasis.

"It was dead before that," insisted Cuthbert. "Its eyes have dropped out."

"What are you trying to say?" snarled Ronald. These two were beginning to remember why they loathed each other.

The Captain scooped up the corpse and threw it out of the window. He could have sworn that someone said, "Thanks, mate", and ran away.

The Captain cleared his throat and announced, "The mill is compromised. Our meetings cannot be kept secret." He paused to get everyone's attention. "Deep Throat pops up whenever he feels like it, the rat was strapped to someone's head and there's a tunnel into the house. We need somewhere else."

Heads lowered and a low muttering began. It was indistinct, but the Captain suspected that it went along the lines of 'not on your life, mate.'

All eyes swivelled to Cuthbert as he cleared his throat. "Obviously, my house is out because Aunt Liza is living there, but we could use the theatre - it's full of furniture anyway at the moment." He paused. And then the solution was obvious. "We could cover it by rehearsing for a play. That way, we could meet regularly and no-one would suspect anything."

Cries of "Brilliant!" mingled with sighs of relief, and the solution was found.

The rest of the meeting was more relaxed until Cuthbert mentioned his search of Aunt Liza's bags. Ronald was instantly smitten. The last thing he wanted in a wife was equipment for manicures and flower arranging, so a bag full of guns appealed to him immensely.

The Captain mused that she may be a highly paid assassin, a femme-fatale on wheels.

Ronald sneered. "Wouldn't it give the game away if somebody built a ramp just before every killing?"

Henry couldn't believe the way his life worked. He found more news stories in this Valley than he ever did as a globe-trotting reporter.

Margery stroked his hand in sympathy.

The Captain barked, "What about you Percy?"

Percy glared from under his hat and snarled, "You'll never get me to talk."

"I thought the problem was stopping you," sniggered Ronald.

The meeting broke up and everyone said goodnight.

Cuthbert and Percy walked home in silence. Cuthbert tried once with, "Are you alright Percy?"

All he received in return was, "Is that one of your trick questions?"

Cuthbert was about to reply when they were both blinded by an intense light pinning them like moths on baize.

"Out rather late aren't we, boys?" The scooter headlight wavered slightly as Aunt Liza hit a subtle bump. She glided silently between them, circled and nudged Cuthbert from behind, herding him forward and separating them. "I thought you would be holding hands at least," she said with a mischievously husky voice.

Cuthbert was stung into asking, "Is it safe for a woman out here in the dark?" He promptly bit his lip as he realised that she was the only predator for miles around.

"There seems to have been quite a meeting," said Liza, voice suddenly sharp. "What's going on?"

As Cuthbert tried to formulate his reply, another voice joined in. "What's going on, Percy?"

Percy had been quite happy to watch Cuthbert's discomfort until the voice purred out of the dark right by his shoulder. Percy fled into the night like a robot with a short circuit.

"We were doing a play," stammered Cuthbert.

"Oh, a play." The voice dripped with derision. "One of your internationally famous plays, eh?"

"Yes." replied Cuthbert, trying to spot Anita in the dark.

"Which one?" snapped Aunt Liza, nudging him with the scooter again.

"Er, we don't know. That's why there was a meeting." He was sidling sideways like a crab away from Liza until he reached a patch of darkness with no stars in it.

"Boo," said Anita.

Cuthbert ran.

Cuthbert found Percy sat up on top of the hill, staring glumly at the construction site spread out below. The huge iron frame was complete and the whole area was bathed in an unnatural halogen glare.

The two sat together in a companionable silence for a while before Percy spoke. "I was hoping to settle here, you know," he began. "Why does everything change?"

Cuthbert didn't know what to say. It hadn't crossed his mind that Percy would move on. He suddenly felt a great sense of impending loss.

Percy continued. "It's my entire fault, you know," he said, glancing at Cuthbert. "A fortune teller predicted that I would wander the earth without rest or reason," he sighed.

'Well, she got the last part right,' thought Cuthbert uncharitably but actually said, "When was this?"

Percy shuffled, which made Cuthbert wary. "As soon as she knew I was an orphan. She predicted that I would be alone in the world." Percy shook his head sadly. "And when I said I couldn't find a job, she predicted that I wouldn't have any money."

Cuthbert couldn't resist this one. "And when she saw the wellies she predicted that you would be a gardener?"

Percy looked at him in astonishment. "Did you go to her too?" he asked.

Cuthbert thought hard and decided that a little clarification would not go amiss. "Which her was this?" he asked.

"Why, the fountain of all knowledge, of course," said Percy with an awed voice.

Cuthbert was puzzled. "Don't you mean 'fount' of all knowledge?"

Percy looked at him pityingly. "Don't be ridiculous. If she sits by a fountain, its self-explanatory, isn't it?"

"Ah," said Cuthbert, "mine was different. What was yours like?"

Percy seemed lost in thought and then spoke with reverence. "She was magical," he began. "She sat on a curved wall with a fountain behind her, and sometimes she answered and sometimes it was the fountain."

"Really?" asked Cuthbert. "How did that work?"

"Well," began Percy shuffling in earnest now. "When I asked her a question, sometimes she would answer and sometimes the fountain would suddenly spurt up to a great height and that meant 'yes', you see?"

Cuthbert was beginning to see. "Aren't those things on timers?" he asked.

Percy scorned him with a look. "Even when she said that I would never amount to anything, the fountain shot up into the sky to say that I would." Percy's eyes were lit by an evangelical fervour.

Cuthbert pointed out, "So even if she was wrong, the fountain was right?"

Percy replied dreamily. "Of course. That's why it's the fountain of all knowledge."

Cuthbert persisted. "And if you didn't like what the Fortune Teller said, you ignored it?"

Percy whispered, "When the water is wise, go with the flow."

Cuthbert snorted. "Well I wouldn't listen to a word of it."

Percy smiled a secret smile and whispered, "Oh ye of little faith!"

Chapter Twenty-Six

The pair of them awoke the next morning to the sound of clattering tracks and tortured metal. They had fallen asleep on the hill-top and they leapt apart expecting Aunt Liza to appear with one of her 'Oh boys' quips.

Down on the site something had happened; one of the huge diggers had fallen into a hole and was trying to dig itself back out.

"The crypt," said Cuthbert remembering his journey through the crypt under the church at Mandrake Hall. He recalled the ancestors lying in state for hundreds of years and now this thing had broken through. "This should stop them," Cuthbert shouted triumphantly. "They can't disturb the graves, can they?"

Without waiting for Percy, Cuthbert ran down the hill to confront Aunt Liza.

Liza was breakfasting on some bird-seed confection, which was nibbled on a daily basis, when Cuthbert burst through the door shouting, "Stop the diggers! Stop the diggers!"

Liza looked at him with those all-seeing green eyes and asked, "Why ever would I do that?"

Percy hurtled through the door, cannoned into Cuthbert and they sprawled across the hearth rug together. "Oh boys," said Liza, shaking her head.

Cuthbert and Percy stood before Liza and babbled like two school boys trying to impress a new Head Teacher.

Liza nibbled at her breakfast and simply watched them until they ran out of breath. "What do you expect me to do?" she asked calmly.

Words tumbled out from the duo before her. "Protected site, excavation, archaeologists and proper research," cropped up several times. Cuthbert and Percy ran out of breath and waited for a reaction.

Aunt Liza nibbled slowly, watching each one in turn before she spoke. "You know boys, that was a really impassioned plea. I agree with you completely. If I thought there was a chance of saving some historical skeletons, I would stop the work right now."

Cuthbert was impressed. Deep down, he knew that she was a beautiful woman, and here at last was proof that she was beautiful inside too.

"Well that's wonderful," said Cuthbert "I can show you the tombs and we can stop the project."

Aunt Liza flicked back her long copper hair and said, "Are you sure of that?"

Cuthbert was clapping Percy on the shoulder and raising a cloud of dust when he said, "Oh yes, they are sat there, just waiting to be discovered."

"Hmm," she said. "Even under all that concrete they're pouring as we speak?"

Cuthbert and Percy ran all the way back up the hill and stopped in their tracks at the sight. A procession of huge concrete trucks was pouring tons of liquid concrete into several holes and trenches all over the site, and behind them more trucks waited their turn, hoppers turning like armoured snails.

"The tunnels," yelled Cuthbert. "They will all be filled in."

They raced downhill to the theatre and Cuthbert pulled the first row of seats apart. Then he grasped the metal plate with the tractor seat on it and tipped it over. Something like dirty porridge lay there just below the surface, heaving gently.

An air bubble burst with an insolent 'pop'.

The two friends slammed the plate back down in disgust and, climbing up to the stage, they slumped into chairs and sank into old springs and depression.

Back at the site, the two women were watching the operation keenly. Anita confided, "It's taking far more concrete than we estimated, you know. It may push us over budget."

Liza reassured her. "It's those damned tunnels. Far better to fill them in. It stops them sneaking about." She smiled. "We don't want to encourage moles, now do we?"

Anita smiled in return and twirled something on her finger. It was a black balaclava and she had one finger in the eye-hole.

Chapter Twenty-Seven

The meeting that night was a strange affair. A black balaclava had been found nailed to the theatre door. There were sinister rumours of people disappearing and concrete being poured.

Ronald grumbled, "Wish I had known they were pouring concrete," looking at Cuthbert.

"You would have known if you hadn't strangled Deep Throat," retorted Cuthbert hotly. "He could hardly tell us after that, could he?"

Ronald narrowed his eyes and other peoples' lives flashed before him, usually at the point where he was ending them.

"Settle down, everybody," shouted Henry. "Bickering with Cuthbert won't solve anything, and murdering him means that we won't have an undertaker any more."

"Don't need one with concrete," muttered Ronald darkly.

Elspeth served tea and actually found herself admiring the two women who had all these men so worried.

"We need a plan of action," barked the Captain. "Got some experience blowing tracks off enemy armour. Should come in handy, eh?"

The others hadn't really thought that war was about to be declared, but now it was out in the open, alternatives seemed few.

The twins had drawn up detailed plans using the school's computer system, planning permission charts and thorough local knowledge.

The Captain surreptitiously slid his pencil line-drawings out of sight under the table when he saw them. One of the twins explained that there had been a delay preparing them due to only having a certain 'window' for the satellite cameras.

Percy wondered why they hadn't simply stood outside to watch the thing but wisely kept his mouth shut. The maps were printed on transparencies so that, as the twins over-laid each one, the assembly could watch the Valley transforming before their eyes.

It was a terrible demonstration of what lay ahead. Even the twins seemed daunted by the size of the task. It wasn't that they couldn't do it. The question was how could they do it with this bunch of old twerps in tow?

"We need more men," announced the Captain and he was relieved when no-one contradicted him.

Henry looked at his brother. "Ronald?" he asked, raising an eyebrow.

Ronald savoured the moment. Somehow this bunch of 'Whim-Whams' always managed to get the better of him, but not this time. "I could put together a private army, of course," he said, "but they won't come cheap, and with all the interesting conflicts in the world, they would probably give this one a miss."

"What about that film?" enquired Elspeth faintly.

"What film?" her husband barked.

Elspeth became flustered as everyone turned to look at her. "Magnificent Devon."

Her husband barked again. "Sounds like a damned travelogue."

"Would someone come all that way to help us?" asked Cuthbert hopefully.

"Hope they only send the cream," said Ronald smugly.

"No, no," said Elspeth. "The villagers were too poor to defend themselves and these seven men helped them for free and saved the village. One of them was bald," she added dreamily.

Her husband the Captain barked in amazement. "That's 'The Magnificent Seven', you foolish woman."

Elspeth cringed under the glares and the giggles and retreated to her teapot in the corner. 'Just you wait,' she thought. 'I may not be alone in this Valley.'

Percy was in the thrall of a revelation. He took off his hat and held it reverently before him. He stood and faced the assembled crowd. "Its destiny," he murmured. Cries of "What?", "Eh?" and "Where?" caused him to snap back, "Destiny." Turning to Cuthbert, he said, "Remember me saying that I had been initiated as a gardener?"

Cuthbert nodded slowly. "Yes, it was the one thing that you would never talk about, if I remember right."

"Well," said Percy screwing his hat tightly in his hands, "my initiation has prepared me for this moment. Has anyone else been initiated?"

Henry looked down at the floor. He had once entered some obscure guild to further his career but he would rather not talk about it.

Ronald, of course, was a follower of Mithras, the God of the Roman soldiers, but he always refused to wear the hat. His initiation had been an utter blood-bath.

Nobody told him the attacks were simulated and he had emerged red in tooth and claw as the only surviving member of the local lodge. Invitations from the other lodges always got lost in the post after that.

Well, he did travel around a bit!

He didn't bother to enlighten this mob and kept silent.

"Thought not," said Percy, crowing. "My initiation involved being taken into a cave and only allowed to wear a gardener's apron and one welly. I was left completely in the dark with a noose around my neck. Eventually they came for me and I had to lie down in a hole in the ground so that I could be pulled back up and reborn. Apparently one of them had a heart attack and I was there for a week. When they pulled me out, everyone was amazed. They said "We've never had one like this before", and "Where's his welly?"."

Percy looked defensive for a moment. "I had to eat something, didn't I? They assumed that I was earmarked for greatness and made me lodge leader, and I was involved in all the great mysteries." He looked around proudly at his audience who resembled an exhibition at Madame Tussauds.

Ronald interrupted with, "What's so mysterious about gardening, then? Dig a hole, plant a plant and then watch it die."

Percy was alarmed. "You said you hadn't been initiated."

Ronald shrugged. "Pure guesswork."

Slightly thrown, Percy continued. "Apparently we all started out as vegetables and there were seven Gods." Percy nodded maniacally so that everyone would appreciate the significance. "Seven," he repeated, "It runs through life like a thread: the seven samurai, the magnificent seven, seven days in a week."

The assemblage began to get it and chimed in with, "seven sisters" and "seven seas." Elspeth contributed, "Seven brides for seven brothers," until she realised that they were all looking at her again and rinsed the teapot.

"You see, the mystic number seven rules everything in gardening," said Percy.

"How?" asked Cuthbert.

Percy had just taken a deep breath to astound them all and was thrown for a moment. "Oh, some plants have seven branches," he said vaguely and tried to continue.

"Which ones?" enquired Cuthbert.

Percy glared at him. "The Menorah tree," he snapped.

Cuthbert was impressed.

Percy had a couple of false starts, waiting to be interrupted again, and then continued. "As an initiate I was able to enter a trance-like state and see into other worlds. Look, I'll show you." With this comment he clambered onto the table and sat cross-legged in the middle. With his arms bent upwards and his hands near to his ears, he began to chant "Ommmmm."

Ronald studied him for a moment and commented, "He looks like an accessory from the Mad Hatter's tea party!"

Percy dropped his hands slowly into his lap and his head fell forwards onto his chest. The humming became deeper and more rhythmic.

"Is he snoring?" asked Henry.

* * *

Cuthbert lay awake, thinking over the events of the day. He heard Percy sneak in after midnight and grumble his way upstairs before slamming his door.

Cuthbert eventually slept, wondering about the other worlds Percy inhabited and whether he could actually tell one from another.

Chapter Twenty-Eight

Cuthbert's dream was shattered by a crashing at the front door. It was light outside and he had slept far too long.

Quickly dressing, he hurried downstairs to find Aunt Liza about to open the front door. The planks of the door were bending inwards with the hammering and Cuthbert almost shouted out, "Be careful," but then he thought, 'What is there out there more terrifying than Aunt Liza?'

Liza opened the door to a patch of darkness with a vertical row of silver buttons. "Constable Beeching, I presume." said Aunt Liza primly. She backed her scooter away and added, "Come on in, Constable. It should be alright, we have widened the doors."

Constable Beeching removed his helmet and tried turning sideways, but he was the same size in all directions. He finally entered using a curious method of threading one arm in first and rotating against the door frame until the other one followed it.

Cuthbert was never pleased to see the Constable. The man had a knack of getting other people to do his work and then arresting them for impersonating a police officer.

"What do you want?" enquired Cuthbert coldly, conscious of Aunt Liza beside him and Percy on the stairs.

The officer puffed out his cheeks in his best pompous bullfrog impression and began. "I have got a body ... "

"Evidently," muttered Aunt Liza, backing further away. The Constable lurched forward and rested his rear end on the kitchen table.

"No, a proper one. We found it in a ditch. A stranger he is."

Aunt Liza zoomed towards him, just stopping at his toe-caps and demanded, "What on earth do you think we might know? How dare you accuse us of anything? Why would anyone bring a body here?"

The policeman looked confused and said, "But Cuthbert is the undertaker, Ma'am."

Aunt Liza backed off again, slightly flustered. "Oh yes, of course, I forgot about his morbid little hobby." Suddenly she was all sunshine and light. The officer was sat down, promised tea and toast, and generally made to feel human. After dumping this problem squarely on Cuthbert, she left for the building site.

Cuthbert and the Constable sat glaring at one another. Percy joined them at the table and asked, "What's this body, then?" stirring at his tea.

"Privileged information," muttered the PC resentfully.

Percy stirred and stared. "I'm privileged," he said, stirring and staring.

The PC dragged his eyes away from Cuthbert and evaluated the figure stirring and staring before him. "Who are you?" asked the PC.

"Undercover," replied Percy.

"And your first name?" asked the PC, removing a notebook. Percy stopped stirring, but the staring intensified. The PC stirred slightly. "Oh, oh, I see." Looking at Cuthbert in desperation, he asked, "Is he?"

"Is he what?" replied Cuthbert.

"Undercover," croaked the PC in a strangled stage whisper.

Cuthbert considered this for a moment and replied with conviction, "Oh, he could be absolutely anything at all."

Cuthbert busied himself preparing the mortuary while Percy and his new friend went for the body.

Cuthbert surveyed his domain and prepared his apparatus. A quick wipe with a cloth and it was pretty much ready. What else was needed but a marble slab and a chap who wouldn't be complaining?

Percy appeared in the doorway with arms and legs hanging over the sides of his wheelbarrow, and the sunlight disappeared as the PC brought up the rear, patting his brow and gasping with the exertion of watching someone work.

Percy tipped the body onto the slab and Cuthbert rearranged the limbs into the standard 'body at rest' pose.

PC Beeching was asking Percy about some of the famous cases he had been on. The PC leaned on the edge of the slab and Percy hopped up to sit beside him, little legs dangling.

Percy began to explain about the Yorkshire Stripper case. "We suspected the triads, of course," he began. "They were known for using all kinds of peculiar muck in their medicines, so when all the trees in Halifax started losing their bark, we all went under cover. Bear in mind that the Chinatown section isn't very big in Halifax, so this was not an easy one."

The PC was so engrossed in listening and Percy was so engrossed in lying that neither of them saw the corpse sit up behind them.

Cuthbert had been fetching plastic buckets and rubber tubing from the house. The old stuff had perished, so he pinched it from Percy's wine-making kit. He would put it back when he had drained all the fluids from the body.

Cuthbert entered the mortuary just as PC Beeching was gasping, "No! After all that surveillance work, it turned out to be a deer?"

Percy nodded seriously and replied, "Either that or a cunning oriental disguise. We never did solve that one."

They both looked up at Cuthbert like two children innocently interrupted at play.

"Well," asked Cuthbert "Where is it? I don't have time to mess about."

The two exchanged baffled looks and shrugs until it occurred to one of them to turn around. "It's gone!" exclaimed PC Beeching.

"So, being a detective really is infectious," observed Cuthbert sarcastically. Dropping his buckets and piping, Cuthbert rushed outside and started to search the out-buildings.

Constable Beeching knew when to scarper, so he made crackling noises and pretended to be called away urgently. Percy sat with his legs dangling, disappointed. He was enjoying himself. That copper had some real potential.

A slight creaking from the far corner made Percy squint in that direction. "Whose there?" he asked.

When something moves in pitch black darkness, it's more of an effect than a vision; there is something, when in fact you see nothing.

Percy realised at once that his meditation last night had produced results. He positioned himself on the table and began the same monotonous hum, eyes closed for concentration and limbs in all the approved positions.

He sensed movement and heard small noises over his humming. Something was approaching, it was close now and Percy willed himself to stay focused in case the spell was broken. With a final 'Ommmm', his eyes sprang open.

The spectre before him was a shapeless mass wearing a crown of silver. Percy felt the thrill of success; he had resurrected one of the Gods. He was omnipotent.

Just then, Cuthbert hit the apparition over the head with a spade. The silver crown, which was actually a stainless steel bowl, spun round and round, almost replicating Percy's hum as it did so, and the resurrected God said, "Ouch!"

Percy was appalled. How do you apologise to a God? Still, if he sat calmly, the God would see that it was nothing to do with him.

"Well done, Percy," said Cuthbert, "You distracted him nicely."

"Oh, thank you very much," muttered Percy already feeling the thunderbolts sizzling in his direction.

Cuthbert whipped the shroud away from the apparition and gasped, "It's the corpse."

The man stood before them rubbing the back of his head and grimacing. "I'm not a corpse. It's me, Deep Throat. The women tried to finish me off. The only way I could escape and see you was to play dead so that I would be brought here."

Still rubbing his head, he sat down.

"Well, you certainly fooled Constable Beeching," said Cuthbert, realising that this was not actually too difficult. "And Percy," he added.

Percy glared. "Who said I was fooled?"

Deep Throat looked at him and said, "Well, it was close when I helped to pull the barrow out of the ditch."

Percy glared at the world in general and climbed off the table muttering, "I was invoking the seven shades. All things are ruled by seven."

Deep Throat rubbed his head again and said ruefully, "Well, you certainly knocked seven bells out of me!"

Percy cheered up a bit at this thought, and spotted the buckets and tubing on the floor. "I use stuff like that for my daffodil wine," he said.

"Do you?" asked Cuthbert innocently. "Well, don't be afraid to borrow some if you ever need it."

Percy was touched. "Thanks, Cuthbert," he said and left the mortuary.

Cuthbert sat down opposite Deep Throat and asked "Why the shroud and the bowl?"

Deep Throat looked a little sheepish. "You had only seen me in disguise. I didn't want you to see my face."

Cuthbert looked at him and said, "But we saw it when Percy brought you in."

"Oh!" said Deep Throat.

Chapter Twenty-Nine

PC Beeching was worried. He couldn't find the relevant papers for 'Corpse in hedgerow', and when he rang Headquarters, no-one seemed to know who Percy was.

Actually, no-one seemed to know who he was either and they threatened to, 'Come and arrest him if he didn't stop mucking about'.

This was a job for an old-fashioned copper. His Mum used to do the washing in an old copper and he planned to hide inside, but he couldn't remember where it was. For want of something to do, he began to idly leaf through his 'Wanted' lists.

The two women were conferring over a flask of rum-laced coffee in a far corner of the building site.

"Can we trust that fool to bury this snooper?" asked Aunt Liza. "I wanted him under the foundations by today."

Anita sipped her coffee and replied, "Well, he was one of our employees and he will be sorely missed. We can visit his coffin to pay our respects and attend the funeral. That way we know that he's properly planted."

She smirked.

Liza nodded her approval and asked, "Who the devil is this Percy?" After sipping her coffee, she added, "Seems a bit of a dark horse."

Anita scoffed, "More of a daft goat!"

Liza thought hard. Anita had a habit of underestimating men. It wouldn't do to relax their guard.

Perhaps she could use some inside help?

Chapter Thirty

Elspeth was dusting when the front door crashed back on its hinges. The shock allowed several dust-motes to escape and drift randomly to the carpet.

"Sorry, I couldn't knock," announced Liza as she glided into the mill kitchen. "It's not easy being a woman and a slave to one's health."

Elspeth gushed her sympathy and understanding. The pathos of a beautiful woman in a wheelchair worked every time. Liza docked beside the farmhouse table and Elspeth fluttered about preparing cups of tea.

Liza dropped the occasional comment about 'women in adversity' and 'immaculate home', and soon they were crouched over their cups like a pair of tigresses over their prey.

Information flowed into Liza's receptors faster than a broad-band connection.

The old adage still held true. In her days of industrial espionage, Liza had lectured her recruits, "Want to know what happened at the Board meeting? Ask the tea lady."

The two were soon firm friends and Liza offered to go shopping with Elspeth some time. Elspeth almost swooned with delight as she said, "Oh yes, please. I have never been in half the shops on your map."

Liza froze. Covering her pause, she fumbled in her basket for a tissue and heard a 'whirring' noise.

"Ooh, that's clever," said Elspeth. "The dog can move its eyes."

* * *

Aunt Liza swept through the village so fast that 'Blind-Pugh' began rounding up the sheep and the dust cloud blotted out the sun.

Anita was startled at the revelations and her mouth set in a firm line as she said, "Men!"

Chapter Thirty-One

The group mingled amongst the furniture on stage as tea and biscuits were served. There was a sense of optimism; Aunt Liza did not seem infallible after all.

Everyone gathered around the table and Ronald asked, "Right, where is the red-devil at the moment?"

A voice from the main door asked, "And what red-devil would that be?" Aunt Liza came silently down the centre aisle with Anita striding purposefully behind her. "Is it a character in your play, Cuthbert?"

Cuthbert looked at the twins, and the twins studied the basket on Liza's scooter. The dog's head was gone. Checking the screen, the twin surmised that it was simply sat in Cuthbert's kitchen staring at the wall.

"Er, yes, it appears after the witches stir the cauldron," Cuthbert said with aplomb, which almost earned him a round of applause.

"Oh, not that Shakespeare nonsense again," spat Liza in contempt. "Translate a three hour play into modern English and it's over in ten minutes."

Everyone gasped; this was blasphemy in the Valley. The Bard was believed to have worked at Mandrake Hall as a teacher and written some of his early works there.

Henry was affronted. "Madam, the words of the Bard … "

" … are piffle!" yelled Aunt Liza.

More gasps. Anita suddenly looked around nervously. There were rather a lot of irate people on the stage at the moment.

Aunt Liza waited until the grumbling stopped and added, "Unless they are properly delivered, of course." She had their attention. "Why don't we all work together to preserve this unique heritage?" she asked in a pleasant tone. "If my projects come in on time, perhaps we could look at a Shakespeare memorial."

Anita relaxed. That was close, but the boss hadn't lost her touch.

"After a few years of profits, we could establish a foundation and build a new theatre." The atmosphere from the stage was electric; dreams were being planted.

People were walking down the stage steps and gathering around Liza as she outlined the future. They all looked around as she waved an arm and asked, "Does this place really do justice to the Bard?"

Neatly executing a three-point turn, Aunt Liza led the potential conspirators away like the Pied Piper clearing Hamelin of rats.

The metaphor was too strong for Cuthbert. He was left with the twins and Percy who suddenly appeared, looked around and asked, "Did I miss anything?"

One of the twins asked, "Why did creepy Ronald go with them?"

"Probably short of ammunition," said Cuthbert, thinking of the bag he had opened. He looked around the table. "Can the four of us stop this thing?"

A variety of shrugs and shakes of the head all added up to one word. 'No!'

Chapter Thirty-Two

Constable Beeching's problem was getting worse.

He knew that he couldn't investigate this murder alone, but should he enlist the help of this chap Percy?

He was still flicking through the 'Wanted' posters when he stopped and looked very carefully at one of the pictures. It couldn't be, could it?

He held the picture up to the light, turned it, and drew a moustache on it. Shaking his head, he rubbed out the moustache, scratched his head and put the picture down again. Then he drew a hat on it.

* * *

Cuthbert was down on his hands and knees, pulling things, prodding things and getting filthy.

The old cooking range was due for a spring-clean, and Cuthbert didn't have a clue what to do. Percy was the mechanical genius when he wanted to be, but apparently this came under 'maintenance', and Percy specialised in 'emergencies'.

Therefore, as Cuthbert turned into a black and white minstrel, Percy sat on the table with his legs swinging, enjoying every moment.

"Did I tell you that one of my ancestors worked on Stephenson's Rocket?" Percy asked.

"No, you didn't," said Cuthbert, spitting out a mouthful of soot.

"Oh well," said Percy, shuffling to get comfortable. "There's a reason why they called it 'rocket', you know."

"It's because it was as much use as a wet lettuce?" suggested Cuthbert, dripping with sarcasm and soot.

The hammering at the door startled them both, and after a fascinating few seconds watching Cuthbert's blood-shot eyes rolling around in his head, Percy asked, "I'll get that, shall I?"

The Constable did his peculiar snake-dance to enter the door and stood there gasping and wheezing. He spotted Cuthbert on his knees and filthy, and pointing at him and wheezing rhythmically, he managed to get an explanation from Percy.

"Oh him. We're doing Cinderella. He's getting into character."

Percy was on top form, regaling the Constable with tales from his mythical past as a detective.

The Constable managed to get his breath back and explained his predicament to Percy. Even Cuthbert crawled out from inside the range to hear better.

Percy scratched his head and said, "Let me get this straight, you caught 'Slippery-Sam' and put him in a cell? He was locked in and you had the only key. The walls are solid; the floor is solid and the ceiling is solid." He paused and arched an eyebrow at Cuthbert. He, in return, shrugged, 'never heard of him'.

The Constable agreed with Percy's assessment of the situation.

Percy went on. "When you got back, he had gone. No visitors, no parcels and no invisibility potion."

"That's right," agreed the Constable.

"And you want me to investigate it?"

The officer nodded humbly.

"Hmmm," Percy stroked his chin like a cross between Sherlock Holmes and one of the hounds of the Baskervilles, and announced, "I need to see the scene of the crime."

The policeman was incredibly relieved and promptly snake-walked out of the door. Percy looked at Cuthbert who shrugged, showing the whites of his eyes and his jazz-hands.

Percy set off after Constable Beeching.

* * *

At the Police station, all was exactly as described.

The cell had iron bars with a door set into them at the front and barred walls at each side. The back wall was of brick and the floor and ceiling were solid concrete.

Percy studied the room from all angles and kicked several bars independently. He then opened the door and entered the cell.

As he stood in the middle looking at the narrow bed and a sink, there was an almighty clang from behind him. Percy turned slowly to see Constable Beeching trying to jump for joy. All the effort achieved was to make ripples travel up and down his chins, but by his standards it was a celebration.

"Got you," he crowed. "Some great detective you are. 'Slippery-Sam', ha! That was a trick, that was, and I got you!" He tried to punch the air, but his heart panicked if his hands went higher than his pockets, so he didn't bother.

Percy sat on the narrow bed and waited for the fun to die down. Eventually he was able to ask. "What precisely am I in here for?"

The Constable flicked through the photos and announced, "Duck stuffing."

Percy stared at him for a while before asking, "What the blazes is 'duck stuffing'?"

The PC wasn't going to relinquish control easily, so he replied, "Wouldn't you like to know?"

"Actually, yes," insisted Percy, "because you cannot charge me with something, if you don't know what it means. That's enshrined in the Magna Carta, that is." Percy sat back with his fingers interlaced, unsettling the Constable with his confidence.

PC Beeching racked his brains for some knowledge of the law, but could only come up with the one about bells on bicycles. This Percy chap was a smart one all right. "Er," he asked, "have you got a bike?"

As the night wore on, Percy settled into a routine. The PC had to provide his food and it was delivered from a takeaway in the next Valley. This was the life, Percy thought: meals on wheels and a twerp on tap!

"Did you know that Cuthbert's family have been undertakers for generations?" he asked after negotiating a strange-shaped bone.

The PC could only shake his head as he tried to mould a cheeseburger into the shape of his face.

"Yep, all the way back to the Pharaohs of Egypt," said Percy.

The PC even stopped chomping for a moment as he took this in. Percy continued, "Back in those days, anyone who knew the secrets of the King's last resting place was buried alive with him. Well, this didn't make sense to Cuthbert's lot, because it took years to train for the job and then somebody slammed a stone door on your fingers and entombed you with the pharaoh. No continuity, you see?"

The PC was staring over his bun, fascinated.

"So, they married into the family who built the pyramids. They, of course, had exactly the same problem - anyone knowing the secret entrance was promptly blocked up behind it – so, between them, they devised a way of leaving small tunnels open to the sky.

The pretence was that every year on the Pharaoh's birthday, the moon would shine on his face and all the Gods would sing 'Happy

Birthday'. Well, this worked a treat until one particular Pharaoh thought that he recognised one of the builders. The Pharaoh had seen this chap get hit on the head by a lump of stone the week before when they sealed his father's tomb, and now he could see a very curious wedge-shaped parting in his hair, and he seemed to stagger a lot.

This caused a crisis. Fortunately, one of the builders' daughters had married a priest, so they had the whole project covered. One of the priests claimed to have had a vision of the Gods walking around amongst the dead King's possessions after the pyramid was sealed - a sort of celestial bring-and-buy sale, if you like.

He revealed that the Gods were half-human and half-animal. From that day onwards, everyone involved inside the tomb at the final ceremony wore a false head. One would have a jackal's head, another that of an eagle, and so on.

This meant that everyone could escape from the pyramid and return to their day job, and if anything should fall off the back of a chariot, well that paid for the next cruise on the Nile. So you see, if you enter an Egyptian tomb even to this day, you can see all Cuthbert's ancestors painted on the walls. It's one of the longest family trees in the world."

The PC hadn't taken a bite in a long time now and his stomach was in despair. He put down his cheeseburger and stared at Percy in open admiration. "How did such a clever fellow as you get involved in duck-stuffing?" he asked.

"Oh that," Percy waved a hand airily. "I had some flyers printed with my photo on and brought them in here when you were on holiday. The other copper said he would advertise my gardening skills if I did him some shopping. His wife had bought a duck because relatives were coming and he left that note so that I would bring the stuffing." He paused. "That's his number at the bottom. Phone him from your car and he'll tell you."

PC Beeching peered closely and said, "I thought that was your charge number."

He got up and lumbered out to the car. Ten minutes later he came back in saying, "You can't fool me, I haven't been on holiday yet," but Percy was gone.

Chapter Thirty-Three

Percy breezed into Cuthbert's kitchen just as breakfast was ready. "Morning, Cuthbert."

"Morning, Percy," Cuthbert replied. "Nice takeaway?"

His friend settled at the table and accepted a plate full of food. Cuthbert watched him fondly as he tucked in. "Still not fixed that key, then?"

Percy mumbled around a mouthful of eggs, "No, it's so twisted now that when he locks the door, it actually unlocks it!"

They both smiled at the thought of PC Beeching scouring the Valley for his fugitive. One thing was certain; he wouldn't think of coming here.

Anita and Liza were in deep discussion in the site office. Anita, buffing her nails, said, "The promise of a new theatre was classic. How long will it keep them quiet?"

Liza checked her reflection as she spoke. "Long enough for us to complete the cinema and the supermarket, then we move on to the next project and they will forget about life before shelf-stacking."

Both women smiled. The projects came and went but the type of people they dealt with seemed to stay the same. Perhaps they should take over a small country next time, just to flex their muscles.

Margery was also checking her reflection. Women did this. She believed because the presence of another woman invited intimacies, if you couldn't have a good gossip with yourself, who could you gossip with?

She reflected that life with Henry, and running the Mandrake Arms, seemed to suit her well enough, but seeing those two successful women made her yearn for the days when she was 'The Godmother' to the Valley-Mafia.

The Valley would be pretty well tied up when this project was complete. A niggling thought troubled her: what if the supermarket introduced drinks cheaper than they could sell them? What would they do if the pub business began to fail?

Margery tapped a long fingernail against the table top. Her twins were quite cultivated now; it would be a shame to get them involved again.

'The Valley-Mafia is a shambles at the moment,' she thought. One lad had been walking around with a rat strapped to the top of his head for so long it looked like the tail of an old Davy Crocket hat.

The fingernail tapped harder. Perhaps she could set up a training camp, get them organized, a new generation of the Valley-Mafia.

The thought inspired her. 'Let the games begin,' she thought.

The twins were thinking along the same lines. They had also seen that the Valley-Mafia had lost its grip on the Valley.

At the moment, they were sat in a library in the next Valley using the internet facility. Looking into Aunt Liza's past business dealings, a pattern was obvious: she moved in, charmed everyone, built a self-financing monstrosity, and moved on again.

'She must have backers,' thought the twins. Where was the money?

They began to scour the Nikkei index for leads to an oriental connection. They were following their own ruling mantra - first question when mugging someone, "Show me the money!"

Henry was also concerned. Life was pretty good. Margery had shown him that hotel-hopping was a young man's game. He had settled down very nicely, but he knew the ways of the world, and Aunt Liza would not be content with a share of the profits. Oh no, Liza was a currency carnivore; she ate money wherever it appeared.

He flicked through his old contact book. 'A few well-placed calls wouldn't hurt,' he thought.

Chapter Thirty-Four

Constable Beeching was poking his migraine with a very sharp stick. He was worried.

If Percy had simply escaped, he could have covered it up, but when he went to the car last night, he left a message on the Chief Inspector's machine relaying the single-handed capture of the notorious duck- stuffer, Percy Plumm.

How did master criminals always manage to escape, he wondered. His migraine rolled over and groaned. He had checked the door and the bars, he had hurled himself at the wall - nothing worked.

He stepped into the cell, remembering a lecture from the Hendon Academy days - "Put yourself inside the mind of a criminal," they had said. "See it from their point of view."

He looked around the cell from the inside and slammed the door. Reaching through the bars, he made sure the key was in the 'unlocked' position and, for effect, threw it across the room.

After ten minutes of being inside the mind and cell of a criminal, he decided that criminals must work up quite an appetite, so he gave up and went to open the door. *Oops.*

His migraine started tugging at his brain, pleading to be let out.

* * *

Elspeth was feeling empowered. Just one meeting with Liza had shown her what a core of steel women really possessed.

Liza was in a wheelchair, for heaven's sake, yet she was in the process of owning the Valley. Nothing was impossible for a woman. What did these men know, anyway? They make a huge noise about world domination, incite everyone to revolution, design and make the most incredible methods of destroying each other, and then lose the keys.

A woman could distract a man in an instant - a certain dress, a smile, a giggle behind a fan, and all his plans of conquest were aimed at her instead.

There was nothing to stop Elspeth having a share of all this power. Why not? Why was she making sandwiches and not ruling the world? "Oh, blast," she muttered, "this loaf is stale," and headed off to Mrs. Biggle's for a fresh one.

Elspeth's husband, the Captain, was also wondering about the Valley and its future. He had settled down here too. The place had some odd-bods, that was for certain, but somehow there was no malice in any of them.

He quite enjoyed being part of an intellectual elite. He wondered if he should dig up his cache of ex-war department explosives and cause some mischief.

Ronald could smell a fight coming from a newspaper headline. He had been using a satellite phone quite a lot these last few days and was calling in favours from all over the world. He had fought in wars and 'emergencies' all over the place.

His main problem over the phone was communication. Face-to-face it was simple: you just shouted and pointed your gun at something vulnerable.

Hence, he had never learned to speak any 'foreign', but things were on their way and he rubbed his hands gleefully.

The milkman looked at his reflection. His permanent outdoor tan seemed to have leaked away into his boots, his hair simply would not flop in a boyish manner, and the sparkle had deserted his teeth.

He had been so depressed that he had missed his milk round twice and nobody seemed to notice. It was as if he was a tradition, not a necessity. He needed a role to play, he needed to be a hero.

It took no skill at all to travel the new roads in the Valley. The horse trotted, he stood. Not even he could make that look heroic.

He matched the stare of the fading star in his mirror and sighed.

Chapter Thirty-Five

The whole Valley had been woken early by a huge helicopter clattering in and settling down on the construction site.

Liza drove up a ramp at the back and Anita strode after her. The machine powered itself into a frenzy and lurched into the air, blowing a dust-cloud kiss behind it.

The Valley in its turn breathed a huge sigh of relief as the thing turned clumsily in the air and flew away.

The meeting that night was very well attended. Everyone came - no apologies were asked or given. They all took a seat and everyone had something to say.

The twins laid out a 'paper trail in progress', charting Liza's company holdings and her associates. The trail had not yet revealed the main backers but the twins were confident enough.

Margery was slightly embarrassed to acknowledge her past role as the 'Godmother' to the Valley-Mafia, but she got into the swing of it and outlined her plan for a new surveillance network.

The Captain joined in enthusiastically and teamed up with Margery to create a para-military force from the available children. Henry looked proudly at his wife, outlined his researches and explained how his contacts could help.

Ronald reassured everyone that supplies were on the way. "Now that we know that Liza is armed, we have entered my territory," he said menacingly.

The milkman assured everyone that he was a 'hero in waiting', and should the call come, he would be there.

Elspeth poured the tea.

Cuthbert sensed that everybody was watching him over the rim of their cups. He contributed, "Bodies won't be a problem."

Everyone relaxed and started to chatter amongst themselves; Percy waited for someone to ask him for his master plan, but no-one did. Eventually he wandered off and sat on the tractor seat to sulk, or as he would have put it, 'Withdraw into himself at the expense of the benefit of others'.

He liked that and reached down into his folded down Wellington for a pencil. As he leaned forward, the base-plate tilted, and as the tractor seat was welded to it, the whole thing fell into a hole.

With a loud, dull clang, Percy found himself sat on the tractor seat on a metal base-plate inside a tunnel. The tunnel began to slide past him.

The brickwork was moving faster and faster over his head and the whole thing was illuminated by sparks thrown up from the smooth concrete floor.

That was it; the concrete Liza had poured into the tunnels had found its own level and simply graded the floor into a smooth Cresta Run. The tunnel system wasn't lost after all.

Somehow the thought was no consolation as Percy hurtled towards wherever the tunnel ended. His life would have normally flashed before his eyes, but no-one had enough time to sort that one out.

The brickwork flashed past and Percy had the distinct impression of traveling through a gun barrel. Back-lit by the sparks, his shadow leapt away in front of him and danced a crazy jig on the walls.

A blast of cold night air announced the end of the tunnel and Percy shot out across a flat expanse for as far as he could see.

Actually 'as far as he could see' was getting closer by the minute.

Percy stuck out one of his Wellingtons, and to the smell of burning rubber he began to spin. "Whooomf, whooomf," Percy's world was now dominated by this strange sound and the centrifugal forces stretching his face around the back of his head.

He stopped; the world didn't. Percy fell flat on his face as his brain refused to stop spinning inside his skull.

Back at the theatre, a crowd had gathered around the hole. The assembled party rightly judged that the concrete had 'self-levelled and probably all run off into the lake.'

They decided that the tunnel system could still be used and they all went home for the night seeing this as a very good omen.

Percy lay watching the heavens spin and convinced himself that he was witnessing creation. PC Beeching began to eat his notebook.

* * *

Aunt Liza's meeting had not gone well. The investors had demanded harsh penalties for any delays.

This was not a problem yet, but any local problems would have to be stamped out ruthlessly.

Realising that her scooter was low on charge, she plugged it straight into the helicopter's rotor system generator and watched with satisfaction as the needle climbed to 'Turbo'.

Anita watched her boss. On the surface, things were fine, but Liza was tense these days. The noise inside the huge helicopter made conversation almost impossible.

Anita decided to look around and keep her options open.

Chapter Thirty-Six

Percy burst into Cuthbert's kitchen the next morning. Cuthbert was just leaving to carry out repairs to the theatre roof and he was a mite distracted.

Percy, on the other hand, was gabbling like an electrocuted baboon. He had set off for home several times in the wrong direction because his head didn't know which way was up, never mind left or right.

He stood swaying and blurting out, "Good news" and "Revelation", along with, "You will never believe it", followed by, "This will change everything".

Cuthbert looked at him and said, "Percy, the concrete didn't fill the tunnels; it all ran away into the lake and the tunnels are clear." He shook his head at his friend and added, "Do try to keep up," and went outside for his ladder.

Percy swayed alone in the kitchen and thought, 'I have been shown the secrets of creation and only I have this knowledge.'

"I am the master of the universe," he said out loud. "I alone, know the things I have seen and I can use this for the ultimate good." His head spun again and he said, "Now, where was I?"

Cuthbert was on top of the barn/theatre roof, nailing planks down when Percy's head appeared over the edge. He seemed more confident somehow, plus he had come to help without being threatened.

Cuthbert finished persuading a badly warped plank that it really should lay flat now that it had several nails in it when he glanced up and saw Percy.

He was walking along the ridge tiles on the highest point of the roof with his arms outstretched. He saw Cuthbert looking at him and gave him a beatific smile. "I think I have gained super powers," he said matter-of-factly.

Cuthbert was never surprised by Percy anymore. "Don't be daft Percy," he said, "Come and help me with this."

Percy held his arms out and there was that smile again. "I can control the weather, summon the thunder."

Cuthbert had to admit that the low rumble he had heard was building up to a full-throated roar. He could hardly hear now and the wind was building up too.

"I can fly!" screamed Percy and flew straight past Cuthbert.

Cuthbert hung on to a hole in the roof as the helicopter roared overhead, flattening him with its downdraft. "Oh Percy," he said as he climbed down to look for him.

The helicopter clattered away towards the building site and Cuthbert walked towards two turned-down wellies sticking up out of the haystack.

The two friends sat with their backs to the haystack. Cuthbert closed his eyes and drowsed. Percy suddenly poked him. "Did you see that?" he asked.

Cuthbert looked around reluctantly, "See what?" he asked.

Percy was pointing, "There, a rabbit just chased a duck along the wall."

"Percy," sighed Cuthbert, "whatever happened to you has left you dizzy. Have a nap and recover."

"Ok," mumbled Percy reluctantly.

Cuthbert dozed, only to be woken again by Percy yelling, "I told you," and sprinting towards the wall.

Cuthbert woke in time to see Percy launch himself over the wall. This was followed by a hideous squeal and a thunder of hooves.

Cuthbert sauntered over to the wall and looked over. A huge pig was thundering off into the distance with Percy clinging on for dear life. Two young lads also stood watching; one had a duck strapped to his head and the other seemed to prefer a rabbit.

"All right, lads?" asked Cuthbert.

"Yes, Mister," they replied, looking downcast.

Cuthbert smiled, "Valley-Mafia?"

They exchanged sullen looks and nodded.

Cuthbert said, "Cheer up lads, I won't tell anyone. You just carry on."

Two scruffy faces brightened and they scampered off shouting, "Thanks, mister".

Cuthbert went back up the ladder to finish the roof. The last plank was almost in place when Cuthbert glanced over at the farm. A cloud of dirty, yellow dust was swirling upwards from the track and coming towards him rapidly.

He shaded his eyes and squinted. Fighting an urge to yell "Twister!" and run for it, he watched a shape leading the cone of dust - Aunt Liza.

Peering carefully over the ridge, Cuthbert watched as Aunt Liza zoomed past the farmhouse and headed for the barn. 'No-one will think of looking for me up here,' he thought.

Liza approached rapidly, with Anita standing on the back, both lots of hair - copper and blonde - streaming out behind them.

Cuthbert expected the clouds to part and the 'Ride of the Valkyries' to blast out from the heavens.

Liza stopped out of sight below him.

'Just keep quiet,' thought Cuthbert as the huge cloud of dust rolled over him.

"Are you there Cuthbert?"

Cuthbert stifled a cough as the dust cloud swirled around him and tried to hold his breath. The dust simply gathered on top of his nose in a pyramid, biding its time. He had to breathe in at some stage.

Aunt Liza was getting impatient. "Cuthbert, where are you?"

Cuthbert was screwing up his face and trying to sift the dust through his nasal hairs when Aunt Liza rammed the barn. The whole thing shook and Cuthbert slid down several planks as he started to cough.

"I know you are up there," yelled Aunt Liza, ramming the wall again.

Cuthbert slid down two more planks. If he hadn't repaired the roof, he could have clung on forever, but another crash from below sent him sliding towards the edge, over the edge, and mid-air into a haystack. With the inevitability of a cartoon, Cuthbert landed safely and glared at the two women.

"You called?" he asked sarcastically. Sat on top of the haystack, he recalled how silly Percy had looked.

"There you are," said Aunt Liza in a waspish tone. "I hear you and that chap who models for 'Scarecrow Weekly' are causing trouble." Her glare demanded an answer.

"Er ... oh, Percy, you mean?" asked Cuthbert, playing for time.

Anita giggled and said, "I call him 'Gingle'."

"Gingle?" asked Cuthbert, thoroughly confused.

Anita clarified the comment with another giggle. "GINger and single," she laughed.

"Oh," replied Cuthbert. "that would make you 'Bingle' then?" he grinned. "You know, blonde ... "

"I know," she snapped and glared at him as only a thwarted blonde Construction Manager can.

Cuthbert was high above them and getting cocky, but his mouth slammed shut as he saw Liza silently line up towards his haystack.

"Don't bother with mine, Cuthbert. Just tell your playmates that the real world has come to the Valley and the real world always wins."

Cuthbert put his hands on his hips. He was too high up to bother about these two. Just as he prepared his retort, Liza zoomed towards the stack and went straight through it.

Cuthbert gasped as he sensed her come out of the other side and his world began to sink. Down he plunged until his feet struck the ground and, as he looked up, the rest of the stack began to fall inwards.

Chapter Thirty-Seven

Margery and the Captain looked at each other and shook their heads; the Valley-Mafia was not an inspiring sight.

They had been dispersed to hide themselves and avoid discovery but every single one of them ascribed to the view that, 'If I can't see them, they can't see me.' So, the Captain simply walked along whacking whichever bit was sticking out. The kids were convinced that he had supernatural powers.

Booby-traps were a disaster. The Captain would let them loose with baling twine, pointed sticks and thunder-flashes, and then go to inspect them.

He approached the first lad who stood to quivering attention and saluted proudly. "How does it work?" barked the Captain.

"Like this, Sir." The lad pulled the string and blew himself up.

As he limped away, the next lad stood to attention and said, "Walk through the gate please, Sir."

The Captain pulled the gate towards him and walked through. "Well?" he asked from the other side.

The lad scratched his head, pushed the gate the other way and blew himself up. Sobbing quietly, he limped off to join his mate.

It was one disaster after another.

The Captain approached a rather robust character standing in a ditch. He was suddenly reminded of a lad in the evasion test, a lad with glasses and a cap. He didn't remember seeing him after that.

"Well," barked the Captain, "how does it work?"

"Would you care to walk along the ditch, Sir?"

The Captain's military instincts kicked in. "No, I bloody well wouldn't. Only a fool would walk through a ditch when there's a perfectly good path," and he strode along the path and promptly blew up.

Margery helped the Captain up and so did the lad in the cap and glasses from the evasion test. The Captain huffed and puffed as he pulled himself together. "Bloody careless, leaving that stuff where someone would walk into it." The Captain peered at the lad and said "Who the devil are you?"

Margery answered, "I have been watching this one, Captain."

The Captain waved her away. "Where's the blighter who blew me up, eh?"

"Here, Sir," said the lad from the ditch.

"Well, where's the lad who evaded us?"

"Here, Sir," said a lad in cap and glasses.

"Good, isn't he?" asked Margery.

The lad quickly removed his cap and glasses and then just as quickly put them back on. The Captain's eyes were falling out with each other. "Stop doing that. What's your name?"

The lad stood proudly to attention, "Jasper, Sir."

The Captain looked him over carefully. "Hmm, Sergeant Jasper, I think, lad," and shook his hand.

Over the next few days, the Valley folk became used to being ambushed on the way to Mrs. Biggle's, or someone shouting, "Bang!" if they tripped a pretend booby-trap; everyone, that is, except Percy who was convinced that the leprechauns had found him and had sent a hit-squad.

Ronald had examined the lake and found that it was now the perfect landing ground for his supplies. The tunnels meant that everything could be hidden in Cuthbert's cellar without anyone seeing and Aunt Liza couldn't get down the stairs to look.

Chapter Thirty-Eight

On the next pitch-black night, Ronald, Cuthbert, Percy, The Captain and some of the Valley-Mafia were standing in a circle on the solid lake.

Ronald was watching one of the kids strangely. The Captain had bet him a fair amount that he couldn't sneak up on this Jasper character and surprise him.

Well, Ronald, of course, was adept at this sort of thing. He utilised every scrap of cover, walked on the balls of his feet, then panther-crawled the last bit before pouncing.

Somehow, he always got the wrong kid. How could he mistake that lad for some twerp in a cap and glasses?

Someone whistled. The plane was coming. Everyone went to their appointed places and held a torch upright, ready to flash it once as the plane passed overhead.

The droning became louder and they could now make out the 'thrum-thrum' of un-synchronised engines.

"That's him," hissed Ronald." One, two, NOW."

Everyone flashed his torch upwards, except Percy who had discovered that if he shone it up his nose he looked like Rudolph, Santa's reindeer.

"Stand back," shouted Ronald. "Here it comes."

A distant whistle became a nerve-wrenching scream and the Captain shouted, "You did specify the right parachute, didn't you?"

Ronald's reply sent them all scrambling for cover. "Parachute? They wanted extra for one of those."

A huge metal container struck the concrete surface of the 'lake'. Sparks flew as the thing struck at an angle and leapt back up into the night over all their heads. "It's heading for the tunnel," someone yelled.

They all rushed after it as it grounded again in a shower of sparks and slid into the tunnel entrance. Everyone crowded around muttering about 'lucky' or 'stupid'.

"How do we open it stuck in there?" asked the Captain.

Percy saw his chance. "Leave this to me," he said, and set off for the farm, torch-beam bobbing about in front of him.

"What can he do?" asked the Captain.

Cuthbert thought for a moment and said, "According to him, anything you like."

He was stopped from commenting further by a distant roar and the sight of two huge torches approaching, both pointing in different directions. "It's Percy's tractor," Cuthbert said reassuringly.

Percy pulled up in a haze of blue diesel smoke and started uncoupling a trailer from behind the tractor containing two tanks, one of oxygen and the other of acetylene. Percy began coupling them together and donned a pair of green glass goggles. When he lit the flame, the green eyes gave him a distinctly threatening look.

"This will only take a minute," announced Percy, grinning demonically in the glare from the oxyacetylene torch. "Nothing can stand in its way. Nothing can stop it."

"Any explosives in there?" asked the Captain calmly.

The torch flame died with a pathetic 'phut', and Percy's eyes lost their green manic gleam. "Well," he said reluctantly, "perhaps that can stop it!"

The next tactic was to tie a chain from the tractor to the container and simply pull it out. The chain was fastened to the container and shackled to the tractor. Percy accelerated amidst great clouds of smoke. The front wheels lifted off the ground and the back wheels sprayed everyone with flayed rubber.

The container didn't budge.

Everyone gathered together as if a huddle of brain cells would somehow connect and produce an idea.

"Well, are there any explosives in it?" asked the Captain.

Ronald mumbled something.

"Speak up, man," barked the Captain. "We'll be here all night."

Ronald gave him the glare which had intimidated its way around the world and said reluctantly, "I don't know. My foreign isn't very good, so I never know what it is in it until it's here." He was scraping one toe in the dirt like a schoolboy.

Everyone stared at him, cleverly keeping their thoughts to themselves.

Cuthbert asked, "Well, where is it from?"

"North Africa," replied Ronald. "Lots of goodies going cheap over there."

A loud crack behind them caused them all to jump and turn around. Percy had lit the acetylene torch again. "Stand back, gentlemen," he said gleefully.

The glaring, jagged flame illuminated his big green goggles and his flaming red hair, but it was the grin which made them all back off.

Percy disappeared in a maelstrom of leaping, sizzling sparks as he turned the immoveable object into molten steel and cut away the end of the giant cylinder.

The flame stopped suddenly as Percy turned off the gas. The only sound was the drip of molten steel onto the concrete.

Pushing up his goggles, Percy reached for a hammer. With a resounding clang, the end dropped off and rattled to a noisy halt like a spun penny, releasing the contents.

About a thousand coconuts rolled out over the concrete lake, rumbling and tumbling in all directions, and clacking against each other like an old men's bowls tournament.

"Coconuts?" exploded the Captain. "Bloody coconuts?"

Ronald looked sheepish. "Nothing wrong with coconuts," he said.

"There is if you are expecting machine guns," ranted the Captain.

Everyone avoided everyone else's eyes as the reality sank in.

Ronald's embarrassment encouraged smothered giggles and then gales of laughter. He stormed off into the night, leaving them to get very daring indeed.

"Don't say anything to Ronald, he'll go nuts!" tried Percy.

"I wonder how much he shelled out for this lot," wondered the Captain.

Cuthbert suggested, "The next play will be the charge of the light brigade. We can simulate the whole charge with this lot!"

Relieved of its load, the container was pulled out and the rest of the night was spent storing the coconuts in Cuthbert's cellar. Ronald didn't come back to help and the coconuts were safely stored away.

The workers sat down and relaxed. Cuthbert handed out bottles of his home-made wine. Even Jasper and his two Valley-Mafia compatriots were allowed a drink. Everyone relaxed and lounged amongst the pyramids of stacked coconuts.

"Hah," barked the Captain, "Looks like the ammunition deck of HMS Victory before a battle." Several more jokes about nuts and shell-shock were aired and everyone laughed too much and for too long.

Cuthbert suddenly thought, 'This is what the Valley used to be like. Nothing serious ever happened here. You made something out of nothing and had a laugh.'

Percy had found some old bits of silver paper and was twisting them into flower-heads.

One of the Valley-Mafia members looked over his shoulder and asked, "What do you do, Mister?"

Percy automatically answered, "Gardener," and carried on twisting his silver flowers into shape.

The young lad persisted, "Bit small for a garden, aren't they, mister?"

Percy looked vaguely annoyed but replied, "Actually, I once had a job in the film industry making miniature flowers and things."

The young lad's eyes widened, "Really? Did you meet anyone famous?"

"Oh, yes," replied Percy, shuffling to get comfortable.

Cuthbert groaned and tried to get up, but he slipped and a pile of coconuts clattered around the cellar floor as he slumped back down.

Percy was comfortable now and he began. "What you don't realise is that when they make a film, it's sometimes shot in the winter and they need it to look like summer." He made sure that everyone was riveted, and proceeded. "I once made three thousand flower heads and stuck them onto the trees to simulate an orchard in summer." He paused to absorb the 'ooh's and 'ahh's' from his audience.

Cuthbert said, "That's incredible. Was the director impressed?"

Percy slumped a bit and replied, "He would have been, but the snow spoilt it a bit." As his audience absorbed that one, he brightened and carried on with, "And sometimes they need everything scaled down. They make models of all the buildings and the cameraman lies on the floor to make it look full-size. They called me in to plant things with miniature leaves to match the scale of the buildings through the camera lens." His audience sighed with respect and leaned closer.

Cuthbert piped up again, "Did that one work?" he asked.

Percy slumped again, "Well it was perfect, but the director postponed shooting the scene, and when the actor entered the shot, the plants had bloomed and the flowers were as big as his head." His audience sighed with regret.

Percy brightened up again, but Cuthbert interrupted with "Percy, do any of your careers last more than a few days?"

Percy glared at him and carried on, "One of the best was a film about the 'Flesh Eating Plants of Mars'. I really went to town on that one. I grafted Venus fly traps with daffodils and scared the cast half to death. Some of the plants were huge. We had to open the skylights to let them out. No-one dared go in at night because the plants started following the guards and stealing chocolate from them."

Cuthbert asked suspiciously, "Any chocolate?"

"Only Mars bars," replied Percy with a straight face.

Cuthbert shook his head, all his worst fears confirmed.

Percy carried on. "The set won awards when we started shooting the film. People came in from all over the world. Unfortunately some of them didn't come out again."

The Captain broke the silence with, "Well, what happened?"

Percy sighed and replied, "The film was closed down and the set locked up permanently after three cameramen disappeared, along with the leading lady. No-one would touch me after that." The audience sighed in sympathy. "Not even when I showed them the postcard from Patagonia with all three of them holding hands with a giant plant."

The audience sighed with the dawning truth and started to mutter ominously.

A voice like a machine-gun firing glass balls at sheet metal interrupted them. "Cuthbert, is that you down there?"

The occupants of the cellar froze. "Cuthbert, are you and your little chums up to something down there?"

Large eyes swivelled towards the stairs as Cuthbert whispered, "She can't get down here. Stay quiet."

The voice stopped and the sounds of scooter-bumping went away. Everyone relaxed and Percy noticed that all eyes were on him again.

He was just starting to feel uncomfortable when the young ears of the Valley-Mafia picked up a distant sound. It was a very faint rumble coming from the direction of the lake.

One of the lads stuck his head into the tunnel, popped back in and asked, "Do we know anyone with a silenced motorbike and hair like fire?"

Everyone jumped to their feet and started to panic. Coconuts were knocked over and people lost their footing as everyone tried to escape in all directions at once.

Jasper took control. "Start rolling coconuts down the slope," he shouted. "Slow her down while we escape through the house."

Everyone changed direction at once, shifting like a shoal of fish and all getting jammed in the access hole in the process. Jasper started pulling bodies out of the way and rolled the first coconuts down the slope.

Soon everyone was rolling them. The clattering built up into the sound of a bowling alley on a Saturday night.

Cuthbert looked through the hole. A headlight was swerving violently from side to side, but still coming. The rider's hair was indeed lit like fire. Nothing stopped Aunt Liza.

Suddenly, only Cuthbert was left. Everyone else had escaped. He massed a pile of coconuts in the hole and delivered one last barrage before he too ran for the stairs.

The clattering, banging noise in the tunnel was supplemented by the wail of a frustrated banshee.

Cuthbert's hair stood on end and he ran.

Chapter Forty

The next morning passed peacefully. Aunt Liza glared at everyone without getting a confession from any of them.

Unfortunately, as she stormed about the kitchen bumping into things, her scooter caught against the old range cooker.

The normal background chugging noise stopped for a moment and Cuthbert held his breath. Liza stared at the contraption and sneered, just as one of the doors flapped down and fired a cloud of soot directly at her.

She disappeared in a black sticky cloud, her flame-red hair amongst all that soot giving the impression of lightning inside a storm cloud.

After ranting at Cuthbert to "Clean that filthy old thing," she stormed out, leaving sooty scooter tracks across the kitchen.

After a discreet giggle with Cuthbert, Percy volunteered to clean out the cooker and all its labyrinthine pipes and flues. Cuthbert explained that he had his own method but Percy would not be deterred, and he began assembling strange looking corkscrew-shaped fittings onto long lengths of screwed pipe.

The background chugging noise increased slightly, like a heartbeat introducing more adrenaline ready for 'fight or flight'.

Percy was oblivious to all this and didn't even see Cuthbert leave the house. As the resident mechanical genius, this was his territory.

Percy was almost ready when Cuthbert returned. The kitchen range watched them carefully. The background noise had reached a steady rhythm and little puffs of smoke could be seen escaping from around the door edges. Percy assembled the last fitting to the last pipe and sat up, satisfied with his preparations.

That's when he turned and saw Cuthbert. His friend stood just inside the door in a dramatic pose with a huge owl on his wrist.

Percy blinked, the owl blinked, Percy blinked, the owl blinked.

Cuthbert coughed to get their attention before the competition became serious. "Stand back, Percy," he said. Percy stood back.

The owl turned its head through 360 degrees to take in its surroundings and to keep an eye on that blinking Percy. The owl was quite content, even though Cuthbert had woken him up when he lifted him from the rafter in the barn. Then it spotted the cooking range and its memory kicked in.

The eyes widened and the wings tried to spread, but Cuthbert had the owl in a practised embrace. Hooking a foot under one of the door handles, Cuthbert flicked open the door of one of the cooler compartments and shoved the owl inside before slamming the door.

The chugging noise paused and then the whole contraption began to give a delighted shiver as it was tickled from within.

Clangs, clonks and clunks accompanied the owl's progress through the cast iron intestines of the cooking range until the owl escaped from the chimney with a relieved hoot, leaving a mushroom cloud of soot over the farmhouse which would gradually settle and add to the patination of the thatch.

Cuthbert looked at Percy with raised eyebrows. Percy sighed, knelt back down and started the laborious process of dismantling his apparatus.

* * *

Liza had showered in one of the site cabins and brushed her hair until it gleamed. Now, she drove onto the site. The building was really coming on. The schedule was tight but all was under control.

She didn't see Jasper standing nearby. He was dressed in an outrageous yellow fisherman's sou'wester. He looked ridiculous when he first put it on and yet, when he stood beside a big yellow digger, he disappeared without trace.

He watched as Liza admired the huge building taking shape before her. The phone in her scooter basket rang with a carillon of hand-bells and she answered it.

After smugly assuring someone that all opposition was firmly under control, she snapped the phone shut. Jasper saw the moment of uncertainty flit across her face and knew that she was not at all sure.

The workmen all stood back respectfully as Liza drove past. They were a hand-picked team who had been involved with her projects for some years.

Whilst everyone was full of respect for her, they were all absolutely terrified of her at the same time; her projects seemed to be her whole world.

Even Anita only seemed to maintain a 'boss and slave' relationship with her. Liza cruised around the site like a shark working up an appetite and she saw everything.

* * *

Cuthbert and Percy sat on top of the hill. Cuthbert watched the new cinema complex take shape and felt the gloom of defeat. "We are not going to win this one, Percy," he moaned.

Percy was chewing on a grass stalk and said wistfully, "Don't be so sure. My old Mum always said, 'Cock of the walk today, feather duster tomorrow'."

Cuthbert looked at him. "She always said that?" he asked. "Nothing else?"

Percy glared at him. "Well of course she said something else. She wouldn't get very far just saying that, would she?"

Cuthbert countered with, "But you said … "

Percy snapped, "I know what I said," and the squabbling began.

* * *

The twins had been trawling financial accounts and tax records of anyone dealing with Liza and her team.

The signs pointed towards a conglomerate of overseas financiers. The question for the twins was 'Where is the profit for us? Do we make money from having a cinema or do we lose opportunities?'

From the details gleaned so far, no-one benefited after Liza's company had visited a location. Trade was monopolised and all profits went abroad, never to be seen again.

The twins began to trawl through the arms catalogues.

Ronald was still smarting from the embarrassment of the coconuts, but he had come up with a plan to fill them with gunpowder and a fuse, and utilise them anyway.

* * *

Cuthbert and Percy returned to the farmhouse and went down to the cellar. "Can you smell burning?" asked Percy.

Cuthbert could and the two ventured into the tunnel to investigate. At the far end, towards the lake, blue sparks could be seen and a hazy, bluish smoke drifted up towards them.

When they reached the concrete lake, it became apparent that Aunt Liza did not take defeat gracefully. A team of her men had welded a huge iron grating over the entrance and she was supervising the operation herself.

Seeing the two appear inside the ironwork, she flashed a set of perfect teeth and shouted to the men to clear away.

When the men had moved out of earshot, Liza waved a large key in front of them. "Sorry, boys," she gloated, "no more nocturnal naughties for you two. This iron grate is tried and tested," and with a laugh she zoomed off into the distance.

Cuthbert scratched his head and turned to Percy. "Does this grate look familiar to you, Percy?"

Percy examined it and declared, "Yep, sure does, Cuthbert. It looks just like my favourite cell door!"

The two of them smirked and went back the way they had come.

Chapter Forty-One

Constable Beeching was counting his money.

He never could resist a beautiful redhead offering him money, even though it had never happened before. There would be no more mysterious escapes.

'Let's see them escape now with no door,' he thought. Then, looking around the room with a bed in the middle, he thought, 'Oops.'

Henry had contacted some of his old colleagues and discovered the same as the twins; Aunt Liza was as big a benefit to a community as a plague of locusts.

Margery was very pleased with herself. Jasper had all the native cunning required to lead the Valley-Mafia. The patrols were coming back with useful information and detailed maps. He also had some unique ideas about sabotage.

The next meeting was very well attended. The twins outlined the dangers to the community and Henry reinforced them. The Captain, Ronald and the Valley-Mafia had been filling coconuts with gunpowder and fuses.

Jasper had loosened the hinge pins from the building site gates. The milkman had been briefed. At last he was given a truly heroic role; he was to lead an overt attack on the site whilst the more subtle sabotage would be carried out during the confusion he created.

* * *

The day came. The milkman's horse stood outside the theatre, stamping and eager to be off, either that or in annoyance at wearing the home-made suit of armour.

The milkman had spent hours flattening hundreds of milk bottle tops and sewing them together before hanging them around his trusty steed in imitation of the war horses of the crusades. The milkman himself had brushed his long golden hair until it was trying to outshine his teeth.

He scanned the crowd for a maiden to sweep off her feet with a last kiss before dying but there was no time - the game was afoot, let battle commence.

He vaulted onto his milk cart, nimbly avoiding two of the Valley-Mafia crouched in the bottom amongst piles of coconuts and a cigarette lighter. With his jaw set towards his goal, he flicked the reins and they took off towards the builders' compound.

Two bushes either side of the gates sprang into action as the dust cloud approached the compound. They pulled the hinge pins out and allowed the gates to fall flat to the ground, still locked together.

The builders were experiencing a moment's quiet as the tea-break began, and they all watched in wonder as a silver-clad stallion roared into their midst, nostrils flaring, eyes aflame and feet the size of meat-plates.

On the cart behind stood the epitome of heroic manhood, braced against all that could be thrown against him.

Then, from either side of him, appeared the Mafia, hurling smoking coconuts into the crowds of men waiting in the tea-line. Coconuts bounced off the men's plastic helmets and exploded amongst them.

Hats, helmets, cups and time sheets flew in all directions. They didn't see many coconuts in the Valley, but it didn't take many explosions to recognise a threat.

Meanwhile, Jasper and a hand-picked elite scuttled among the parked vehicles. Clambering up onto the diggers and excavators, they lifted the flap on the vertical exhaust pipes and dropped short lengths of wooden broom handles down them.

Another team started loosening hydraulic pipes and releasing the oil. The huge buckets lowered wearily to the ground with a sigh as the oil ran into the ground.

As the milkman herded the workers over to the far end of the compound, one of the Mafia shoved a broom handle through the door handle of the Site Office, trapping the occupants.

Jasper himself had commandeered a digger and was advancing on the Site Office from the side. He slid the front edge of the bucket underneath the building and lifted it bodily.

The whole Site Office became airborne and was placed directly on top of a similar building. Aunt Liza and Anita found they were stranded one floor up.

The Mafia began to celebrate. The milkman completed his circuit and rejoined them grinning from ear to ear as they all congratulated each other.

A crash from the direction of the Site Office stopped all the back-slapping immediately. Aunt Liza had driven her scooter straight through the Site Office wall and hit the ground in front of them.

The scooter landed heavily and the shock caused the headlight to switch on and hang loose out of its fitting. The suspension had sagged with the impact and the wheels were sunk into the soil.

Aunt Liza, however, was immaculate. Her hair flamed, her eyes flamed and she threw a switch. The scooter seemed to rise as its suspension stiffened and it crouched there like a fighting bull, its cyclopean eye swinging wildly. The wheels spun, the dirt flew, and so did Liza, straight at them.

The Valley-Mafia executed a perfect 'bomb-burst' and dispersed in all directions. The milkman's horse, remembering a wild night with a one-eyed mare, hesitated for a fatal moment and lost its cart and part of its tail. Then it joined the exodus to the gate, with the milkman skiing behind with a coconut jammed under each foot, one of which was smoking suspiciously.

Aunt Liza tore after them like Boadicea pursuing the Romans; more than coconuts were going to roll for this.

As Liza almost caught the milkman, one of his 'skis' blew up, showering her with soil and gravel. She stopped to wipe her eyes and the milkman zoomed through the gates, allowing the Mafia to swing them back into place and put the hinge pins back in.

The sound of Liza's threats receded as the intrepid band of saboteurs made their way back to the village.

The adrenaline was still pumping and the milkman was now a genuine hero to a new generation in the Valley.

Chapter Forty-Two

People slept where they fell that day; everyone was exhausted. The main entertainment involved sitting on the hillside watching the mechanics try to start the bright yellow beasts below.

In all the confusion of explosions smelling of coconut oil, no-one had seen Jasper's party trick dropping wooden staves down the exhausts.

This effectively stopped the engines without showing a fault anywhere in the mechanisms. Large lumps of mechanical innards lay about.

Curses were hurled, helmets were kicked and spanners thrown. When none of this worked, all they could do was sulk and blame the foreign workers who put the thing together in the first place.

Liza roared around, throwing up dust and hurling insults. Every time she came upon a shattered coconut shell, she glared up at the hillside, squinting to see who was there.

She knew where the nuts had been stored, now she had to catch the nuts who had stored them.

Percy came looking for Cuthbert. "Look what I've found," he said.

Cuthbert looked around to see a stringy looking chap with long hair tamed by a sweatband, carrying a guitar and wearing a poncho. Cuthbert shook his head. "The hippie festival is in the next Valley and you've missed it."

The chap gave his guitar a gentle strum and replied, "Oh that's alright, I always miss it. Avoids the crowds, you see." He sat down beside Cuthbert and stared into the Valley below. Percy sat down with them and told Cuthbert how he had met his new friend, and filled him in on what was happening in the Valley.

"Does he have a name?" asked Cuthbert.

Percy beamed and replied. "They call him 'Banjo'."

Cuthbert looked at Percy, then looked at the newcomer and asked, "Why?"

Percy was astonished. "Isn't it obvious?" he gasped.

"Not when he plays a guitar, no," observed Cuthbert.

That argument had great potential for an afternoon's entertainment, but it was interrupted by a musical moment beginning to form beside them.

"She's a redhead, hmm." Strum. "The scooter's red, hmm." Strum. "Both scary, hmmm." Strum.

'Banjo' adopted a deep gravely voice and began:

They were made to do a job, and they did it well.
Then one of them escaped from the gates of hell.
They called it red.

Strum.

All eyes turned to Banjo. This was good. He was immediately invited into the fold. After all, Robin Hood had ballads written about him; why not the Valley-Mafia?

* * *

Liza had problems. It was as if the investors had a spy in the camp. They had rung twice this morning, just as everything was going wrong and the machines had broken down.

She had to make the men make loud growling noises in the background and keep clanking metal plates together to simulate working diggers.

One idiot clonked coconut shells together, prompting the voice on the phone to demand that she, "Get that track-rod end fixed."

Liza was not happy. She paid these fools to protect the machines. They had dealt with sabotage before and yet they seemed lost for an explanation this time.

She spun her scooter in a vicious, tight circle and headed towards the temporary site cabin, the one on the bottom of the stack.

Jasper eased away from the bulldozer he had hidden against, reversed his yellow storm coat and left via a hole in the fence.

Reporting to Cuthbert and the others, he could confirm that all progress was halted and that the phone calls were getting heated.

One of the twins radioed the news to his brother. The other twin immediately hacked into a company main-frame in Hong-Kong and arranged an extraordinary shareholders' meeting as soon as possible to discuss problems with the Valley project.

Liza's phone began to ring.

Trucks had been rolling in for days now. Some of the diggers had been stripped down to the chassis and still weren't working.

Liza had simply moved the emphasis to the building itself. The walls were being assembled and the seats were being installed. It was like trying to stop water; block it in one place and it simply flowed around you.

* * *

The meeting that night was a tricky one.

The whole Valley was celebrating the success of 'Cuthbert's Raiders' who were even immortalised in song by Banjo, the hippie troubadour.

However, the fact was the cinema was becoming a reality. It was now a huge building and looking more solid every day.

The Captain was sulking. He had tried to follow military tradition by scheduling a raid for '02:00' hours and was met with blank looks. It was even worse when he tried 'Two o'clock in the morning.' No-one in the Valley even realised that there was a two that far down on the dial.

Henry had taken over the chair and Percy had taken over the clock. He had removed the clock face and innards from the Grandfather clock, and when the Captain had been speaking, he allowed the front glass to swing open, revealing him gurning just over his shoulder.

Henry waited until two volunteers lowered the clock down flat to the floor, trapping Percy inside, before he spoke. "We have done remarkably well so far, but I am afraid that Aunt Liza has raced ahead with her schedule. The building must be the main target."

He paused to check several sheets of briefing notes and continued, "Our scouts report that all security has been strengthened and cameras installed all around the compound. Liza herself has taken to sleeping on site, and around-the-clock patrols have been established. He paused and surveyed the assembly, "Has anyone any ideas?"

Ronald stood up, strode to the front and slapped a pointer against the map on the easel. "Three men," he announced, "here," slap, "here," slap, "and here," slap. Each one has a rocket launcher and they zero onto the building. We synchronise the firing and vaporise the thing."

The room was stunned. Was it really that simple? Hands were poised to clap when Henry asked, "Do we have any rocket launchers?"

Ronald glared and mumbled, "No."

Henry persisted. "Three men who know how to fire them?" No reply. "Do we even have three watches to synchronise?"

Ronald slouched his way back to his chair. An incredible crashing and clanging came from behind Henry as Percy escaped from the clock.

"Coconuts," he shouted.

"Oh good Lord," muttered Henry.

"No," said Percy eagerly, "we can fire coconuts at the building."

Muttering began amongst the audience, heads nodded and people agreed with him.

"Can we throw them that far?" asked Cuthbert.

Percy beamed. "Leave it to me," he said and stomped off in his turned-down wellies to prepare.

Ronald snorted. "I give them rocket launchers and he offers coconuts," storming off in disgust.

Henry watched them go. Percy, Cuthbert and Jasper - all the available brain power in this room and they had handed control to the three stooges. His attention was caught by a murmur from the back row. A huddle of women were getting quite excited about something.

"Margery," he called "what's going on?" His wife, Margery, reluctantly came to the front with a poster in her hand and bashfully handed it up to Henry.

Henry read out aloud, "Special first night preview, 'Lost Souls of the Amazon', starring Monty Blissett and Stephanie Squirms." He lowered the poster in amazement and asked, "Are they really ready for a preview?"

"They must be," replied Margery. These have appeared all over town. Somebody said that Monty and Stephanie will attend on a red carpet."

The other women appeared to swoon.

Henry crumpled the poster in his hand and slumped down in his chair. 'Bring on the stooges,' he thought.

Chapter Forty-Three

Percy was in his element, Jasper was a willing apprentice and Cuthbert was watching his farmhouse being dismantled.

One of the barns was now an ordnance factory, with rows of tables manned by the Valley-Mafia sawing the tops off coconuts and pouring gunpowder into them before gluing the tops back on and inserting fuses.

Percy and Jasper were lining up the tractor and fitting lengths of drainpipe to the exhaust pipe.

It was starting to look like the devils harmonium.

The theory was, explained Percy, the exhaust pipe would pump gasses into the tubes where the pressure would build up and fire a barrage of bombs at the cinema over the hill. Apparently this could only be achieved by experimenting all night and wearing one's cap backwards.

Everyone gathered around as Percy sat high up on the tractor, adjusting the revs and building up the exhaust gases in the twelve tubes fitted behind him. The tractor was lifted off the ground and the wheels spun freely. All was set.

Percy gunned the engine. The improvised pressure gauge spun around like a magnet dropped at the North Pole, the tubes were loaded and the fuses were lit.

Percy jumped up and down with glee.

The tractor roared, the fuses hissed. The crowd backed off. Percy gunned the engine to a scream. The fuses hissed, the crowd ran.

Percy stood on the pedal.

"Boomph!" The first missile left the tube, followed by each other one consecutively. Sparks streamed across the sky as the fuses sucked greedily from the atmosphere.

The sparks described a curve as gravity insisted upon reclaiming its coconuts and they headed for ground zero. The first explosion was a muffled thing, quickly followed by the others.

One of the twins stepped away from the cheering so that he could hear his brother on the walkie-talkie. Waiting for a pause, he announced sombrely. "We have destroyed the pub, the Post Office and the crossroads."

The villagers looked at him in horror. Even Percy looked less than pleased.

The twin continued, "Sorry, couldn't resist that," grinning all over his face. "We landed a creeping barrage across the offices and into the cinema."

Everyone cheered and Percy was hauled onto several shoulders and paraded around. The night belonged to them but who knew what the morning would bring?

Chapter Forty-Four

The morning actually brought a mutinous building crew and a crow with tinnitus.

The workers were revolting and they advanced upon the Site Office like pitchfork-wielding villagers. Anita poked her head out of the door and quickly withdrew. The men assembled in time-honoured 'angry-mob' formation and muttered loudly.

The Site Office doors crashed open and Aunt Liza was amongst them. The muttering stopped. Driving slowly and silently among them, Liza made eye contact with every one of them. Not one man managed to maintain that contact.

She circled the group and came to an intimidating halt in front of them. "How many of you were with me when we knocked down the children's home and built a vital trolley park for the supermarket?"

A few hands crept up but all eyes stayed down.

"How many of you were with me when we faced down a whole order of nuns so we could knock down the convent and extend the council's rose garden?"

A few more hands went up and some started to make eye contact again. Liza met the eyes of some of her most stalwart workers. "You, Sid, did you flinch when the mother superior swung her rosary at you? No."

Her gaze swept the throng. "Charlie, I remember you limping after all those school children kicked your ankles black and blue, but you soon came back for more."

Backs began to stiffen and a glint of pride started to appear. Liza cruised up and down in front of them.

"Some of you have been involved in 'Black Ops' with me, dangerous jobs abroad where no-one would have acknowledged our existence if we had failed." She stopped before them again. "Who remembers the battle of the Temple of Bells?"

Several men stood rigidly to attention and some wiped a tear from their eyes. "That thing had stood for a thousand years but my team had it flattened in a weekend. The sweat-shops we built have supplied all your overalls ever since. We lost good men on that day. Are we going to forget their sacrifice?" She paused. "Those men became Buddhists because they didn't have what it takes to be part of 'Team Liza'." All the men were at attention now. "Are we going to let these Valley turnip-heads beat us?" she screamed.

The men roared, "No."

"Will we complete on time?"

"Yes," they roared.

Liza smiled and lowered her voice slightly. "I may be only a feeble, disabled woman," she paused for pathos, "but I have a scooter that can flatten anyone who gets in my way."

The men roared their support and streamed away to start repairing last night's damage.

Anita appeared at her side, "I don't know how you do it. I thought we'd lost them that time."

Liza looked unusually thoughtful before saying, "If we are late with this building, we'll lose more than our builders."

Chapter Forty-Five

Back at the theatre, Percy was the man of the hour. Even the Captain and Henry had given the floor over to him.

Margery asked, "Have you always been so ingenious, Percy?"

"Oh yes," said Percy, shuffling to get comfortable. "I was responsible for an automated production line when I first started work."

Everyone gathered around and hung on to every word.

Percy waited for everyone to be seated and for someone to stop coughing at the back, then he began. "Production lines had been established during the wars to speed up production, but in the modern age it all needed revamping. Well, my firm got the contract at the local sweet factory, but as soon as we arrived the foreman had an accident."

"What sort of accident?" came a question from the floor.

Percy looked around for Cuthbert suspiciously, and replied, "Well, the Foreman was standing on top of one of the big mixing vats, looking down to see why the paddles weren't working. He sent me for some tools and then asked for a ladder. Well, it was noisy in there and I thought he said 'adder'. We found his cap and scrapped the whole production of fudge for that day, but never did find him." Percy readjusted himself, wriggled and continued. "Anyway, the production line was next door. That's where a line of girls packed the different chocolates into the boxes. Each girl had a different selection dropping down a chute beside her and they popped them into the compartments as the boxes went past. Well, I commandeered a shed on the side of the building and looped a drive belt into the factory to power the conveyor belt. All was well, and the girls speeded up to match the new demands, but it was boring, so I introduced music through loud speakers and it helped to keep a rhythm going. Everybody was happy and I was about to be promoted."

A voice, suspiciously like Cuthbert's, again came from the floor, "What happened, Percy?"

Percy glared into the crowd but couldn't spot his tormentor, so he continued, "Someone changed the band-wave on the radio to pick up some more modern songs. One of the 'latest hits' involved clapping along. 'If you are happy and you know it, clap your hands (clap-clap);

if you are happy and you know it, clap your hands (clap-clap)', and so on. Well, every time the girls clapped, the boxes moved on and by the end they were half-empty. Everybody was yelling to reverse the drive belt to bring the boxes back but it wasn't designed that way. The Boss and some of the labourers got hold of the belt and pulled as hard as they could in the opposite direction, strangling the donkey. And that was the end of that."

Percy sighed and hung his head. After watching his cut-down wellies swinging below him for a while, he looked up. Everyone had gone.

Percy smirked and wandered off in the general direction of the house. The night was clear and Percy looked up at the stars. He remembered a game he used to play when he was a kid.

He stood with his arms out wide and looked straight up. The stars seemed to be moving in a curve, as if he could see the spin of the earth. As his arms grew heavy, Percy raised them until they were horizontal again.

That's when someone grabbed both arms and put a bag over his head.

The sky went black and Percy felt himself being lifted from both sides and hurried away. Now, Percy's head had been in a bag before when it had been any old bag the twins could find at the time.

This was almost a designer bag for kidnappers. He could breathe and there was a faint, elusive scent. Where had he smelled that before?

His eyes widened, or at least he thought they did - it was still dark. "Aunt Liza," he whispered. Percy began to shake.

* * *

Cuthbert had said goodnight to everyone as they left.

They had all been in that sort of stupor which always follows one of Percy's tales, so not much was said. When he turned around, Percy was gone.

After locking the theatre, Cuthbert spotted Percy on the farm track, standing with his arms outstretched.

"Jesus," muttered Cuthbert, "and on my farm too". He looked around guiltily. His parents had always been very strict about blaspheming.

When he next focused on the track, Percy had been hoisted between two giant builders and his cut-down wellies were pedalling an invisible bicycle.

Cuthbert ran to the farm.

Since Liza had moved out, the twins had installed a high-tech alarm system which would rouse the Valley-Mafia in seconds. Cuthbert burst into the farm and pressed the large red button by the door. Nothing. No wail of sirens, no fireworks, no electricity.

Cuthbert slapped his forehead and promptly regretted it. The twins had forgotten one tiny detail.

When the lights came on in the Valley, it was usually to celebrate the lights coming on in the Valley, that's why the building site had its own generators.

He dashed up to the bedroom and hauled out his father's blunderbuss. Dashing across the yard, he aimed in the direction of the old church tower.

The blast knocked Cuthbert off his feet. A tongue of flame lashed out into the night and various nuts, bolts and old spanners hurtled towards the old church bell.

The crow had been fast asleep in the tower. It was out of the draught when the bats had left for the night, and in his dreams his top-hat gleamed and his footwork was entrancing all the birds. The old bell suddenly boomed out right next to him and several spanners began to ricochet around inside the square tower.

Spitfires had never scrambled as fast as the crow did. He was in the air and battle-ready before his feathers had warmed up. He hurtled towards the only target in sight, slightly ironic in this case.

Blind-Pugh had shot upright onto all four legs at the commotion. He knew not for whom the bell tolled, but the crow flew for him.

The crow's beak thudded into Blind-Pugh's rump and the sheepdog took off into town. Straight as an arrow he went. Trying to turn corners with this speed and his eyesight was never an option anyway.

Constable Beeching had just flicked on his indicator and turned slowly into the High Street. He liked driving through town in the dark. No-one could see the pile of takeaways on the passenger seat for a start.

The black and white sheepdog flashed across in front of the police car and Constable Beeching wrenched at the wheel, hitting the kerb and flipping four steaming trays into his own lap.

Bumping along the pavement, scattering cats and litter bins, the police car headed for the Mandrake Arms at speed.

A console flashed in the twins' bedroom. They had installed a device in the constable's car, running from its battery. It sent out a signal as soon as the car approached and alerted them to his presence.

One twin leapt to the window upstairs at the Mandrake Arms and the other activated the defences. By pulling various ropes, two large ornamental tubs moved across the doorway outside and the hanging baskets lowered themselves to head height.

The police car crashed into the ornamental tubs without touching the building. Constable Beeching's door flew open and dumped him onto the floor, steaming and dripping as the tin-foil dishes cushioned his fall.

He struggled up and knocked himself out on a hanging basket. The twins came down and surveyed the scene.

One twin wiped a finger on the constable's helmet and stated, "Hmm, No. 34 and a No. 56. Odd choice!"

The other twin looked over to the skyline where a smudge of grey smoke from Cuthbert's blunderbuss still hung in the air against the night sky.

"That's either coming from the farm or the old mill," he announced. "Primitive alarm system but effective. Wonder why he didn't just push the red button?"

The other twin added, "Trouble at t'mill, eh lad?"

The twins began to run.

Chapter Forty-Six

Percy was startled when the bag was pulled from his head. The Site Office was brightly lit and he blinked to adjust his eyes.

Liza sat opposite him with a tray of gleaming steel implements before her. Percy gulped. Could he withstand torture, he wondered. Already knowing the answer gave him no comfort at all.

Liza nodded to someone behind him, footsteps retreated and the door shut. They were alone.

Percy went on the offensive. "You can torture me all you like," he yelled defiantly. "Any coward can torture a man when he's tied to a chair."

Liza stared calmly back at him. "Are you tied to a chair?" she asked.

Percy lifted his arms. "Oh," he said. He tried again. "Don't think I'm scared of your torture implements either."

Liza sighed, finished cleaning her nails and put the implement down before picking up another to begin filing her nails.

"Oh," said Percy.

Liza took her time with the manicure, glancing up at Percy every now and again. The tension mounted. Percy noticed that all the backpacks from Liza's scooter were stacked along the wall behind her in a row. He also remembered what was in them.

Percy needed to talk. He was only Percy when he was talking; silence unnerved him. "I'm not really a gardener, you know," he tried.

Liza never missed a stroke with the file. "Really?" she said, the green eyes melting him slightly before sliding back to the job in hand.

"No," Percy rushed on, sensing an opening. "I'm undercover, you see." He watched to see if this made an impression; it didn't. "People will be looking for me." Percy put on his most convincing display of nonchalance. "Any minute now, men in balaclavas will come crashing through the walls and windows."

Liza's eyes opened wide. "Goodness me," she said. "Will I need a big strong man to protect me?"

Percy waggled his shoulders in a primitive display of masculinity and opened his mouth, but Liza interrupted, "By the way, do you remember the last man in a balaclava who came to the Valley?"

Percy closed his mouth.

The twins ran through the village flinging gravel at all the relevant windows. The Valley-Mafia was lurching into action and a tail-back of sleepy-eyed youths began to form up behind them as they headed for Cuthbert's farm.

Percy was actually starting to relax. Aunt Liza had melted him with a smile as she said, "Do you realise that we are both on wheels now, Percy?" It was the first time she had used his name.

Percy looked down, blushing slightly and saw what she meant. He gave a little whoop and spun around on the office chair before pushing off and rolling across the floor on its castors.

Liza smiled at him and he blushed to a deeper shade of crimson. "I wonder what else we have in common," she mused.

Percy was smitten. He watched as Liza's mobile phone twittered and she picked it up. He saw the way she flicked her long red tresses over her shoulder and the way her lips parted as she spoke into the phone.

A door opened and Anita entered. Percy received another dazzling smile as she laid down a tray of coffee and biscuits before leaving. Percy watched the steam rise from the cups and wondered whether to pour or not.

Just then an ant appeared trekking across the table and heading for the tray. Percy watched as a whole column appeared, marching up the table leg from the floor. He didn't like to brush them off and he certainly wasn't going to interrupt Liza, so he just watched.

The lead ant carried out a complicated inverted manoeuvre to climb up and over the rim of the tray and the rest followed. The lead ant made straight for the bowl of sugar lumps with the silver spoon in it.

The ants disappeared behind the rim and Percy watched in amazement as the spoon tipped over to rest against the rim of one of the cups.

He could almost hear the effort as a sugar lump appeared slowly over the rim and slid along the spoon, plopping into the cup.

An ant ran along the spoon and checked the delivery before scuttling back along to the bowl where another lump was being raised. The next lump slid neatly into the cup and the ants stood poised and waiting.

Liza seemed to notice them for the first time and paused from her conversation. Leaning over slightly, she pursed her lips and blew. The ants scattered across the table and onto the floor where they dispersed in all directions as Liza continued with her call.

Percy was impressed; this was a seriously spooky lady.

Cuthbert had briefed the assembly at the farm and the Valley-Mafia went into a huddle. The main thought seemed to be, 'Would they have got out of bed if they had known it was only Percy in trouble?'

Jasper took control, with the blessing of the twins, and split his forces. Half would assault the main gates with skateboards and ramps, while the other half would use the tunnel system.

After the target was snatched, everyone would escape through the tunnels which were now nicely graded all the way to the concrete lake.

Watches were synchronised, except for Egbert's; his Mickey Mouse had lost an arm so he would have to follow everyone else.

Cuthbert watched them disperse into the night and sighed. It seemed to be a young man's game these days, he thought as he headed back inside. The crow glared at him as he passed. He had spent the last ten minutes jammed into a knot-hole in the fence and had been spinning around trying to get the twist out of his beak.

Liza finished her call whilst absently stirring her coffee. Closing her phone with a snap, she turned to Percy. "Sorry about that Percy," she purred, "now where were we?"

Percy's eyes had been straying to the ranks of large, square containers against one wall. They were the back-packs from Aunt Liza's scooter, and thanks to Cuthbert, Percy knew what was in one of them.

Liza narrowed her eyes as she watched him and hissed, "Why don't you look inside?"

Percy's eyes swivelled like a gimbal in a gale but he walked over to them and hesitated before unzipping a bag fitted out with a full picnic set, including decanter.

Liza hissed again, "Try the one on the left. That's the one your idiot friend spotted."

Percy's hands shook as he grasped the zip. The front cover was gradually peeling down and the butts of several lethal weapons began to show. Percy's hair follicles were vibrating in panic until he looked closer and exclaimed "What the ... ?"

"Hair-driers, Percy. My collection of portable hair-driers. A girl has to look her best, you know." She fixed Percy with a steely stare and snapped, "Sit down and forget everything that fool 'Custard' has told you. In fact, tell me more about this rescue you have been imagining."

Percy quickly sat and began to simper as her green eyes gave him their full attention.

Suddenly her eyes widened in shock. The door burst open. The room was full of small men in balaclavas and Percy was whisked backwards at an alarming rate and the door slammed shut again.

"Goodness me," she whispered. "I thought he was bluffing."

Percy's voice had frozen in his throat. He hurtled down the ramp from the office and was literally swallowed up by the earth.

Next thing he knew was the effect of hurtling through a dark pipe surrounded by whooping banshees on skateboards with lights on their heads. The noise of all those wheels in the confined space was unbelievable.

They all zoomed downhill into the darkness, with the skateboarders using the tunnel as a pipe and carrying out dizzying stunts around Percy who felt like a neutron in an atomic reaction.

Percy stuck his little legs out in front of him so that his turned-down wellies would take any impact, and he was quite stable until someone patted him on his back, causing him to spin.

This was too much. Percy was trapped inside a kaleidoscope of light and noise until he reached the hole in Cuthbert's cellar wall. An arm reached out, grabbed him and dumped him unceremoniously on the floor.

Jasper and Cuthbert exchanged satisfied looks. The Valley-Mafia rumbled off down the tunnel and Percy was safe. Percy sat in a daze trying to focus on the two blurred forms on each side of him, then, recognising the voices, said "What did you do that for? She was eating out of my hand."

"Standard Percy," muttered Cuthbert as he went up the steps with Jasper, leaving Percy trying to get his balance back.

Percy spent some time weaving about like a man trying to plait his own legs before jamming himself into a corner and falling asleep.

Chapter Forty-Seven

Whatever it was waking Cuthbert the next morning, it certainly wasn't a cock crowing. Obviously, the crow was still having trouble with his beak.

After breakfasting alone and carrying out the routine farmyard duties, Cuthbert wandered down into the Village. It didn't matter what time he got up, there was always a queue at the Post-Office, and it was always the same people.

Billy 'Bottom' Whyper, the odd-job man, would be depositing handfuls of coins paid to him the day before, the village gossip would be tuning her hearing aid which Cuthbert was convinced was a parabolic reflector because she never missed anything, and they would be greeted by two little old ladies who manned the Post-Office queues all over the globe.

"'Ow are you this morning then, duck?" began the first old lady. "'Ow's life treating you?"

The thinner one of the two sighed and shook her head. "Had the fire brigade out last night again," she said.

"Again? What happened this time?" asked her friend.

"Chip pan. Had it twenty years and it suddenly goes up in flames."

More head shaking as the whole queue joined in sending a ripple through the line like a Mexican wave.

The first old lady patted her friend's arm and asked, "Flame up too high?"

The victim was aghast. "Oh no, global warning."

The queue leaned slightly inward towards the source of this revelation.

"Things just burst into flame nowadays because of that global warming. Last week it was our 'Arrys bed. He nearly choked on his fag, he did."

The queue began a synchronised nodding routine in sympathy as someone else joined in. "Wait 'til all that ice melts then. We'll have penguins here then."

"Where, in here?" asked someone in alarm.

Someone else chimed in, "Hope not. This bloody queue's long enough as it is."

Cuthbert only heard half of these revelations as he was staring at a gaudy poster on the wall. Aunt Liza was advertising the coming film season; it made him realise that time was running out.

"Better hold a meeting tonight at the theatre," he muttered under his breath. "We need everybody there this time." And he walked out into the street. The grapevine would spread the message and it was much cheaper than buying stamps.

Two hundred yards further on, Margery called out, "Meeting tonight, Cuthbert. See you later, then," Cuthbert smiled.

The meeting was packed. The hum of conversation and the smell of stewed tea met Cuthbert at the doors of the theatre. Everyone seemed grouped by gender tonight.

The men were clustered together in one spot and the women clucked excitedly around the tea urn.

Cuthbert half-expected Percy to be standing under a sign announcing 'Gardeners' like some strange hotel convention. Squeezing between the groups, Cuthbert could hear snatches of conversation.

"That Harry Hemlock could come through my window, anytime;" twittered one of the crowd.

"If only Monty Blissett would come and rescue me," said another.

The men's group was noisier, without actually saying much at all - something like "Stephanie Squirms, eh?", followed by a nudge and a wink, seemed to convey far more information than all the words used by the women.

"Ooh, look!" shrieked one of the women, staring at the stage. Everyone looked and gasped as a small figure appeared staggering across the stage, bandaged from head to foot.

"Is it Harry Hemlock?" asked someone.

"Is it alive?" asked someone else.

"Is it Percy?" asked Cuthbert.

The hat on top of the bandaged head was a dead give-away as the caricature mummy gave a muffled yelp and fell off the stage.

Jasper appeared with some of the Valley-Mafia. "Hope you don't mind, Cuthbert. We sustained a few minor injuries last night, so I started a first aid course for the lads."

The crowd gave a relieved giggle and resumed its background babble.

Jasper stood beside Cuthbert and explained. "We practised on Percy because he was the cause of most of it." He grinned.

Cuthbert returned his grin and added, "Always gets wrapped up in a new subject, does Percy."

Cuthbert climbed the steps and walked onto the stage. Some of his furniture had been taken back to the farmhouse since Liza moved out, but several pieces seemed to have elected to stay on as props.

Gazing over the heads of the assembly, Cuthbert felt a warm glow. He had never had this many friends before. He knew them all and they had shared adventures, so the conversation never seemed to falter whenever a group met together.

He scanned the crowd. Even Banjo, Percy's hippy friend, was there. Margery and Henry still exchanged fond glances across the room.

The twins were huddled together with Jasper, and the milkman was circulating, trying to discover his part if the theatre ever staged another play.

Percy was thrashing about just out of sight and the old lady with her hair in a bun was knitting away happily.

Cuthbert spotted Elspeth happily providing tea and cakes to Mrs. Biggle from the Post Office, and Belinda the barmaid was following in the milkman's wake like one of those tiny fish who follow a shark.

Right at the back was the old lady knitting away. Cuthbert started. He could have sworn that she had been on the front row.

All the front row seats were now taken and he recognised everyone; he stared hard at the old lady in the middle of the fourth row knitting away patiently. 'How did she get there?' he thought. In fact, who was she?

Someone called out, "Come on, Cuthbert. You look as if you've seen a ghost."

Cuthbert concentrated. What a thing to say to an undertaker. His mind did a quick scrolling inventory but he couldn't place her. Plenty of little old ladies, of course, but he didn't recall any of them knitting.

Cuthbert scanned the sea of faces and was so distracted that his usual nerves disappeared and he welcomed everyone to the meeting.

"We don't have long before the cinema opens. We have all seen the posters and the builders are moving rows of seats in as we speak."

Cuthbert groaned as the theatre doors crashed open to announce the arrival of Aunt Liza and her fellow Valkyrie, Anita.

Skidding to a halt at the front, Liza addressed the audience. "Oh good," she began. "If Cuthbert's still speaking, I won't have missed anything." She carefully examined all the faces before her. "What is this, a rehearsal?" she asked innocently.

"Er, yes," replied Cuthbert quickly. "It's for the new play."

"Hmm," Liza mused, cruising up and down before them all. "Could be interesting. Is there a role for me?"

No-one replied and all eyes swivelled desperately to Cuthbert who stammered, "Er, we did consider you, of course, but there are steps up to the stage," he finished lamely.

Liza studied him before replying. "How sweet, and here was me thinking that perhaps you assumed that I couldn't act."

She cruised silently to a spot just in front of Percy who had managed to free one arm and now had his eyes showing. Liza threw back her hair and pointed a wavering, elegant finger directly at him.

The audience expected lightning to crackle from the finger tip to the tip of Percy's nose as she spoke in a voice dripping with menace and foreboding. "If I ever come face-to-face with you again, you will feel the wrath of generations of warrior blood, and hear the accumulated battle cries as they descend from Valhalla to wreak my vengeance."

Before a transfixed audience and Percy's crossed eyes, she grabbed a loose bandage and reversed her scooter so fast that Percy span around like a top. At the end of her travel, Liza pulled hard on the strip of bandage and Percy began to spin in the opposite direction, coming to a halt in front of her again.

"Be gone, foul sprite!" she screamed, "before I summon the legions of the damned to assail you with the bows and arrows of a woman scorned."

Percy gave one last whimper and hobbled rapidly away like an earthworm in a one-legged race.

Liza beamed at her audience and said sweetly, "You see, nothing to it."

The stunned silence was broken by a slow clapping sound. One member of the audience was daring to clap in the most insolent manner possible. Aunt Liza's nostrils flared as she strained to see over everyone's heads to find the culprit.

Cuthbert watched as the old lady slowly rose to her feet, sliding a knitting needle into her bun as she stood. Cuthbert was close enough to hear Liza gasp and whisper, "Nanny", before waving sharply to Anita and racing for the exit, leaving behind a stunned silence.

Cuthbert kept an eye on the old lady. She never seemed to be where you last saw her.

After stalking silently, Cuthbert managed to corner the woman near to the tea queue. "Hello," he began," I'm Cuthbert."

The old lady peered up at him and her gaze returned to her knitting. 'Clickety-click, clickety-clack' went the needles. "I know who you are, my dear. I saw you many times when I was Nanny to her Majesty." 'Clickety, clickety, clickety, click'.

"That's incredible," gushed, Cuthbert, "Were you really Nanny to...."

"Oh no, dear not that one. I was Nanny to Queen Liza the First," she interrupted, clicking furiously without looking up.

Cuthbert tried another tack. "You must have some tales to tell about Aunt Liza, then?" he suggested.

She glanced upwards, almost in panic, and then her eyes returned to her knitting again. "Oh no, dear, nannies never gossip. That's an unwritten rule, that is. Never reveal anything about an employer, dear."

Cuthbert looked at the needles flashing under the stage lights. It was a wonder the wool didn't catch fire. A vague feeling was creeping over Cuthbert as he heard the rhythmic clicking.

Somehow it seemed to suggest that the clicking was more important than the words. Glancing around for moral support, Cuthbert spotted the twins over by the wall. One had his hand cupped to his ear and the other was writing furiously in a notebook. Jasper had been positioned across the theatre and was scanning the crowd urgently.

Spotting Cuthbert, he ran over to him and whispered, "The twins are intercepting messages. Someone is trying to contact us."

Cuthbert was trying to remember which expression he used to make when he wanted people to give up and walk away, but a hand dropped on his shoulder.

"Damned clever that, Cuthbert, how do you do it?" asked the Captain.

Ah, he remembered this response, "Do what, Captain?"

"Well, send Morse code at that speed. I haven't heard anything like it since my service days. Damned impressive."

Cuthbert saw the twins closing in, and when everyone was gathered, he introduced them. "Gentlemen, this is Aunt Liza's nanny. She's very discreet but I think she has something to tell us."

* * *

The theatre meeting had broken up and a new one was taking place around Cuthbert's kitchen table.

Nanny sat at one end, knitting away quite slowly this time so that the twins and the Captain could keep pace. Sheets of paper were scattered about, covered in hasty shorthand ready for translation.

The Captain puffed out his cheeks and leant back in his seat. "From what I can make out, Liza has sunk a lot of people's money into this project.

She carried out a hatchet-job on the Board and took over the company. This project is the one which will make or break her reputation. No wonder she's tense."

"Tense," snarled Ronald. "She even makes me nervous."

Cuthbert spoke for everyone when he asked, "Is there anything there we can use to stop her?"

The twins looked up and shrugged, obviously facing a night of hard work, and continued writing. Nanny gave him a sympathetic look and carried on clacking.

The door opened and in breezed Percy. "What's all this?" he asked, perching on a corner of the table like a bean-bag garden gnome.

"Morse code," muttered a twin, not bothering to look at him.

"Never!" exclaimed Percy. "That brings back memories."

Even Nanny stopped clicking for a moment as everyone looked at Percy.

The Captain broke first and asked, "You know Morse code?"

Percy looked around the table as if slightly offended. "Of course. How else do you talk to another submarine?"

Nanny started clicking slowly again. The twins kept their heads down.

This time it was Ronald who had a momentary lapse of judgment. "You were never in submarines," he sneered.

Percy swung his little legs for a while and asked, "Then how do I know about HMS Dolphin?"

The Captain gasped and Ronald went quite white.

Ronald murmured darkly, "No-one knows about HMS Dolphin unless ... "

" ... they were there," supplied the Captain.

All eyes were now on Percy who sat there swinging his legs without a care in the world.

Cuthbert broke the deadlock with, "If somebody doesn't ask him, we will be still sat here when Liza celebrates her tenth anniversary in the Valley cinema business."

Nanny clicked rapidly for a few seconds and the Captain said, "Nanny says, if you don't soon tell us, she will stab the nearest warm body with a knitting needle."

Chairs scraped away from Nanny as Percy shuffled to get comfortable. Cuthbert groaned in chorus along with all the other long-standing Valley residents currently in the room.

Sat on the corner of the table, Percy had his back to most of them, so he drew up a chair, shuffled again and began. "Submarines can't just chat away to each other or flash lights to pass messages. They spend most of the time underwater and radio only works when they surface. But if you tap on the side of the hull, the sound travels through the water and can be heard by another submarine as clear as a bell. That's why they 'run silent' when another sub is nearby. The whole idea is to sneak about without anybody knowing where you are. That way, if somebody needed a nasty surprise, we would pop up and give it to them."

Percy scanned his audience, saw the rapt attention he desired and continued, "Morse code consists of dots and dashes, each permutation denoting a different letter. It can be sent by wire or tapped out on a hard surface. If we knew that a friendly submarine was nearby, we could tap on our hull and they could hear us and reply."

Ronald interrupted. "So you were in the Dolphin?" he asked.

Percy paused before continuing. "No, I was in 'Dasher'. We often went on patrol together. My mate Cyril was in the Dolphin. Everybody had their own signature with Morse code. You could tell who was on duty by the way they operated the key or the way they tapped."

The Captain leaned forward eagerly. "Do you know what happened to the Dolphin? It's one of the great sea mysteries."

Percy suddenly looked concerned. "Look, I have never spoken of this before and I will deny all knowledge of it if I'm asked again."

He shuffled silently and continued. "Both boats set off together this particular day. We dived just outside the harbour mouth and changed course underwater. The skipper came over on the tannoy to tell us that we were on a secret mission and all the rocket silos were armed. The rumour was that we were the first strike capability team and if something kicked off, we would start World War III. These two nuclear submarines carried enough warheads to settle the matter once and for all."

Percy leaned back in his chair and noted the silence. The needles had stopped knitting, the twins had stopped writing and Ronald was no longer sneering. Cuthbert was hiding behind his neutral face and Elspeth was ignoring the boiling kettle.

He continued. "Out in the mid-Atlantic we had an urgent message from the Dolphin. They thought that someone had smuggled poison gas on board to sabotage the mission. After searching the vessel from stem to stern, they found my wellies in a kit-bag; Cyril had picked my bag up by mistake and I had his squash kit. Anyway, the Captain decided to fire them out of a torpedo tube."

Ronald exploded. "What the devil did you have wellies on a submarine for?"

Percy looked affronted and replied, "So I could look smart when we went ashore on leave."

He carried on. "The wellies expanded in the tube and got stuck, so Cyril tapped out a message to me asking our Captain for advice. The Captain came down and told us that the emergency books were in the Dolphin's safe. Ours had pages missing after the steersman was caught using it for cigarette papers, so it was no use now. The Captain ordered me to send the message 'Dasher don't know - open safe - sign on dotted line - dash to tubes - fire.' Well, apart from the confusion of tapping out dots and dashes to say dotted and dasher, a maintenance man was tapping pipes to check for a leak in the engine room. Cyril actually received, 'Dasher will blow - unsafe - enemy on line – fire.' Dolphin reacted immediately and fired its acoustic warheads, all designed to home in on the nearest sound. This happened to be Cyril tapping out, 'Are you sure?', and that was the last we heard of them."

The clack of knitting needles broke the silence, gradually becoming a staccato rattle, and everyone in the room understood that message.

Chapter Forty-Eight

Inside the cavernous space of the new theatre, things were tense.

Liza was charging up and down the aisles like a robotic sheepdog, herding workers into a space or out of a corner, and keeping everyone moving.

Anita had tried to ask why they had left the meeting early last night, but Liza had ignored her.

The Site Manager tucked a tendril of blonde hair back under her yellow helmet and watched carefully. This was a huge project and all their futures depended upon it. If there was a problem, she had the right to know.

The inside of the huge shell was swarming with workers. Yellow hats bobbed about like a Wordsworth poem as rows of seats were positioned and bolted down.

Scaffolding covered the interior walls as fake opera house boxes were added. The idea was to create a retro image similar to 'La Scala' in Milan.

This was supposed to fool the audience into thinking that they were enjoying 'culture' instead of a night at the 'flicks'. Gilded cherubs stood patiently against a wall, waiting to be hoisted aloft and stapled to the walls at strategic points - much quicker than hand-crafting them in situ, thought Anita.

The ceiling already had a gigantic chandelier hanging from the centre. It hung there, dark and threatening, like some colonic growth, but when a switch was thrown, it would glitter and sparkle like all the other illusions created in the room below.

The work was back on schedule but it had been a close call. Cuthbert's band of circus clowns had been a nuisance but they seemed to have run out of steam.

Anita strolled back into the foyer where the first pickings machines were being installed. These were designed for the children and teenagers who were sent to amuse themselves as the parent queued.

The queues would move slowly enough for junior to pass level one on the game and demand more money for level two as the queue crept forward. Then came the food supplies and drinks, all at child height and presented in very bright colours.

The entrance aisles were narrow here to slow the people down and let junior see what he was missing.

Anita thought back to the dark, rainy days of her youth when hiding in the cinema for a free second viewing was the only way to avoid the reality outside.

Modern cinemas had thought of that too. The seats were so damned uncomfortable that some people would never see how a film ended.

She toured the site and went outside to watch the deliveries. Why did things running smoothly make her so suspicious?

* * *

Cuthbert pondered the subtle changes creeping over the Valley. The meetings were less well attended and he could swear that people were avoiding him.

Posters for the new film première were everywhere. Rumour had it that the two big name stars were attending personally. Harry Hemlock was already in London and Stephanie Squirms was flying in from somewhere expensive abroad.

Cuthbert sat on his stile, face tipped upwards to the warmth of the sun, and tried to think of a strategy. If he really thought hard, he would have to admit that he was curious about all this film business himself.

The theatre had always been a passion in the Valley. Perhaps it was time for a change. Cuthbert smiled a secret smile.

His imagination had just provided an image of him directing his theatre group in a movie - 'The Borgias', starring Margery and the twins, or 'Ben Hur', starring the milkman and his cart.

There would be difficult scenes ,of course; anything involving Percy walking in a straight line for a start.

The crow stood nearby on top of the water pump and tilted his head as he watched Cuthbert.

People thought that birds like him tilted their heads to get a better view; the truth was he was a slave to his sinuses and it was the only way to keep them clear.

141

He blamed the beak bending collisions he was suffering lately. Somehow, Cuthbert was never far away when they happened, which was a good reason to keep an eye on him.

The crow had studied people intently for as long as he had lived in the Valley. There wasn't an awful lot to do around here on long summer days.

Food wasn't a real problem because Cuthbert had some fantasy about running a farm and all sorts of stuff was left out for animals that no-one had seen in years.

He only hired a horse when he needed one and yet he put bales of hay out every week. At least when it piled up and became a haystack, it started to look like a farm. Apparently Cuthbert dealt with all the dead people around here as well. In birdland, when you couldn't fly, you died, and when you died, you disappeared. Simple!

Actually, the crow was privy to one of nature's secrets: the animal kingdom had its undertaker too.

Many a dark night, the crow had spotted the local fox carrying an inert flop of feathers away into the distance. No fuss, no bother; all this performance humans went to was beyond him.

This business of putting people into the ground had exercised the great bird-minds for generations; the practice of putting stone slabs up on top of them was really intriguing.

At the last great telephone line conference, all the aerial survey results had been collated. Squadrons of birds had flown in faithful grid patterns for months, charting the patterns as seen from the air.

Sometimes a pattern would emerge and then someone would build a road right through the middle of it. Another group had hopped from stone to stone in various sequences to see if they were buttons waiting to be pressed.

All the conferences had degenerated into screeching matches and resulted in hundreds of delegates all wheeling chaotically about before going home in disgust.

Some even migrated abroad to seek other opinions. Whoever solved this riddle would really feather his nest.

Chapter Forty-Nine

The dreaded day was here. Aunt Liza's cinema was holding its première tonight.

The whole Valley was in a state of excitement. Groups gathered at street corners and people moved apart sheepishly as Cuthbert came near.

He didn't really notice. Cuthbert was wrestling with a desire to see this new phenomenon in action himself.

Excitement really is contagious, and finding Percy's wellies polished outside his bedroom door meant that he would be sat at home alone if he didn't join in.

A burst of fireworks over the cinema announced the opening of its doors. Giant spotlights shone upwards to illuminate a tethered gas-filled balloon looming over the proceedings, silent and ghostly, as it relayed birds-eye views of the gathering crowds threading their ways to the red carpet leading inside.

Attendance tonight was free, so any problems of conscience were neatly put aside. Crowds of strangers holding cameras lined the path to the door awaiting the celebrities.

Each end of the red carpet was firmly anchored down after Anita had convinced Liza that a practice run would be a good idea. Liza had been positioned at the doors on her gleaming scooter and a sweaty workman, picked at random, had stepped down from his dumper truck and begun to sashay along the carpet.

Liza had driven forward to greet him and the back wheels had gripped the carpet a little too fiercely and whipped it out from under the workman's feet. The man crashed to the ground, shaking the foundations, and the carpet was spat out behind Liza to end up in the foyer in a tangled heap. Several practice runs later, all was ready.

A limousine slid silently into place at the end of the carpet and the crowd hushed respectfully. It was the longest car ever seen in the Valley. It looked as if they were made in giant lengths and someone had forgotten to cut it into sections.

The limousine driver came around to the side and opened the door with a flourish, and hesitated as a barrage of words hit him from inside the car. Flushing with embarrassment, the driver bent his knees until he was as tall as the occupant of the car.

Harry Hemlock stepped out of the limousine and flashed a smile at the world, waving with one hand as he moved along the red carpet, swivelling as he did so to present his profile in all directions at once.

Behind him, the driver straightened up to his normal height and muttered his way back to his driver's seat.

Harry Hemlock was in his element. He had perfected a technique for the modern age of fan worship. He would approach fans of a similar height to himself and pose with them as they took a photo on their mobile phone for posterity

Approaching the wall of fans, he chose Mrs. Biggle from the Post Office. She looked harmless and she was small. Throwing an arm around her, he shouted, "Camera", and beamed at the spot where the miniature appliance should appear.

Now, as we know, progress arrived late in the Valley and not everyone was at home when it came. Mrs. Biggle hoisted her trusty Kodak and pressed the button.

Harry Hemlock yelped as a set of bellows shot out and smacked him full on the lips. He quickly put some distance between himself and this side of the crowd, bumping into the opposite wall of fans.

Recovering his composure, he turned and was confronted with Percy in a ghoul mask with a hat on top, trying to get into the spirit of things.

Harry yelped again and made for the doors, only to be faced by Liza accelerating rapidly towards him bearing a huge bunch of flowers. His nerve broke and he ran inside to hide, gibbering behind a cardboard cut-out of himself.

The crowd thought he was re-enacting one of his scenes and applauded wildly.

The arrival of another unlikely-shaped vehicle caused an expectant hush. The driver opened the door and a vision emerged. She smiled at the driver and nodded her thanks. S

he stood and shimmered. Her dress shimmered, her hair shimmered and she moved but no-one saw how. She was at one side of the crowd, smiling, as she avoided a kiss and then she was halfway along the carpet on the other side, chucking Percy under the chin and giggling the next.

The crowd was entranced. Stephanie Squirms worked the crowd, accepted the bunch of flowers from Liza, passed them to her assistant, and entered the building without a pause or any interruption to her shimmer. The crowd all exhaled together and started to enter the building behind the celebrities.

Several different films were showing simultaneously on the opening night. Cuthbert had sneaked in last off and been the first one out.

He had watched a very complicated plot about betrayal and revenge, all of which could have been avoided if the man had said 'Sorry' in the first place.

If Valley folk behaved like that, Cuthbert wouldn't have any time for farming.

He waited outside and watched as the audiences filed out. The twins and various cohorts of the Valley-Mafia came out at a run, slapping the rumps of imaginary horses as the film still coursed through their imaginations like adrenaline.

Margery was supported by Henry and they had obviously watched the weepy where Stephanie Squirms had played an extraordinarily glamorous munitions worker on the poverty line with eight children and a terminal illness. And she even managed to survive!

Percy was mock sword-fighting with Jasper as they re-fought the battles of Captain Bloodlust of the Thames Estuary, and Ronald lurked in the shadows, taking advantage of all natural cover as he evaded the men in black from some secret organisation at the tax office.

Cuthbert was depressed. The theatre would cease to exist overnight. He had never seen any of his audiences walking away shouting lines from 'The Merchant of Venice', although he had disturbed one or two Romeo and Juliet moments when he was locking up.

Chapter Fifty

Cuthbert joined the Post Office queue the next morning. The conversation was taken up entirely by last night's event.

Hairstyles had changed overnight and strange transatlantic words had entered the Valley's vocabulary. Mrs. Biggle had pinned an enlarged close-up photo of Harry Hemlock's bruised lips on the notice board for everyone to envy.

Elspeth seemed to be attempting to shimmer; her dress was a departure from her usual 'Frump-Chic' and, on closer inspection, seemed to be made from bubble-wrap.

Cuthbert shuffled forward like a reluctant member of a chain gang. 'This was the future,' he thought. No more Valley gossip, no more farming tips or weather warnings.

All conversation would revolve around the latest release and 'Who wore what whilst doing which to whom' in last night's movie.

Cuthbert accepted his purchase silently as Mrs. Biggle talked over his head to someone more interesting, and he left the shop.

The journey home was miserable. All anyone asked as he passed by was, "Did you see ... last night?". Anyone watching a different film to the enquirer was dismissed as belonging to another tribe, and ignored.

Cuthbert was glad to arrive home, until he spotted Percy that was. Several chickens scurrying from the theatre alerted Cuthbert to something amiss.

As Cuthbert entered the theatre, Percy swished past him on the end of a rope. There was a brief impression of a spotted bandana and an eye-patch attached to a bloodthirsty scream as Percy whistled past.

The rope caught the top of the doorway, Percy lost his grip and went bowling down the farm track like tumbleweed in last night's movie.

Henry stood patiently and ticked some boxes on his clip-board. "Next," he shouted.

Cuthbert took in the line of people waiting around the theatre and approached Henry. "What's going on?" he asked.

Henry replied absently without looking up, "Grab the rope, swing across the theatre and try to land in the gallery up there. Jump to it - people waiting."

Cuthbert looked up at the worm-eaten ledge which had been mysteriously re-named 'The gallery', and let out a polite cough.

Henry sighed at the distraction but smiled when he saw who it was. "Cuthbert," he beamed, "glad you're joining in the spirit of things. Grab the rope. Percy seems to have done with it for now."

Cuthbert stepped back as the next in line grabbed the rope and ran up onto the stage. Henry looked keenly at Cuthbert, "Not entering the stuntman auditions, then?"

Cuthbert walked away.

Once again, the air in Cuthbert's kitchen hummed with ideas. Unfortunately, none of them were his and he didn't like any of them either.

Henry was speaking in a pleading tone. "Look, Cuthbert, the theatre is in the past. I have contacts in the business. We can get hold of cameras and set up our own film company. We will all have jobs and be millionaires."

Everyone was nodding away around the table as if suddenly making movies was in everyone's grasp and they should simply do it. Elspeth had rustled up some snacks in the kitchen, mostly beans and hot-dogs, and she busied herself clearing the table.

Percy had been unusually quiet and it caused everyone to keep sneaking a look at him, wondering what might be in store for tonight.

Gradually the table cleared, except for the sauce bottles, and almost all of the people present had fallen silent. A meeting just wasn't the same without Percy's contribution.

Cuthbert took the hint and asked, "Anything you would like to say, Percy?"

Percy looked around suspiciously, before saying, "Careful, walls have ears."

Ronald laughed out loud. "An old dump like this probably has eyes, ears and little scratchy feet too."

Elspeth yelped and moved closer to the Captain who spluttered, "What are you getting at, Percy?"

Percy leaned across the table and said in a low voice, "You people forget. I have been in the nerve-centre. I could have sabotaged all

Liza's sophisticated equipment, but someone," he glared at Cuthbert, "pulled me out and wrecked the plan."

It was Cuthbert's turn to laugh. "So your plan involved strange men throwing a bag over your head and carrying you off, even though you didn't know who they were, where they were going or when it would happen?"

Percy put a finger to his lips and looked around again. "Watch and learn, Cuthbert," and, quick as a flash, he snatched up the ketchup and HP bottles off the table, and threw them out of the window. "There," he said sitting back smugly, "now we can talk."

Ronald spoke slowly when he asked, "What the devil are you doing, Percy?"

Percy looked around the table in astonishment, "You lot are real amateurs, aren't you? How many times have you read that the 'information came from unknown sauces?"

There was a thud as Cuthbert's head hit the table top. Reality had simply refused to support him any longer.

Percy ploughed ahead. "She must have been listening in for years. How did she know where to build the cinema, eh?"

The Captain replied. "She inherited the land with Cuthbert."

Percy hesitated, but not for long. "Why did she build it right just there, then, eh?"

Ronald contributed, "Because that's where the Hall stood when it burned down, Percy."

After a moment's hesitation, Percy came back with, "All right, then, how did she know we would all go to see the films?"

Three people all answered at once. "Because it was free, Percy."

"Oh," said Percy, slightly deflated. "You can see what made me suspicious, though, can't you?"

Ronald addressed the table at large with, "Well, even a broken clock is right twice a day!"

Chapter Fifty-One

Cuthbert slept in for the first time in years. The Valley no longer seemed to have a social life; everything revolved around the cinema.

No-one came to the meetings anymore; they were all stupefied by the cinema they were supposed to be shutting down.

Cuthbert stretched luxuriously in the old feather bed and idly scratched his ear. Remembering Ronald's comment about 'Little scratchy feet', he looked around suspiciously and got up.

He swung the window out, scraping it against the thatch, and stared longingly at the old barn converted into a theatre.

No-one wanted to rehearse now; no-one had the time. There was always another new film due in town, or a special feature, or a matinee to fill the gap between the pensioners' morning show and the adults evening necessity. Conversation included film stars as if they were neighbours and everyone nodded sagely at their rumoured antics.

Cuthbert dressed slowly and noticed that even the cows in the next field had congregated in the corner nearest the cinema as if they were watching the latest offering. Whatever they would make of screeching tyres and gunshots, he could only imagine.

The farmyard was deserted. Even the malignant crow seemed to have somewhere better to be. Cuthbert wandered around his kingdom, idly kicking a broken coconut shell out of his way.

He had forgotten about the coconut grenade launcher. The tractor still sat up on blocks to let the wheels spin free, and the iron tubes were still connected to the exhaust pipe. Cuthbert thought that there were even some coconut bombs left in the out-building somewhere.

As he went to look, he suddenly realised he was the Valley undertaker; people weren't even dying anymore. They probably didn't want to miss Stephanie Squirms tied to a post - yet again - while some stuffed gorilla tore up bonsai trees in its rage.

Cuthbert glanced at the pile of coconut bombs and then across to the tractor. He thought for a moment and glanced each way again. 'Why not?' he thought. The cinema would be empty at this time in the morning and perhaps people would get back to normal.

Collecting an armful of projectiles, he stumbled across to the tractor, dropping them with a clatter as he climbed up to look for the keys.

The crow was snoring merrily, head tucked under his wing, his favourite dream playing out in his head. It was the one where he was wearing his top-hat and smoothing out his tail. This old pipe he had lodged in was working very well for him. It was warm from the sun and out of the draught.

A faint clatter disturbed him and he immediately suspected Cuthbert. Opening one eye, he peered up at the circle of sky above him and tried to hold onto his place in the dream.

The noise went away and he drifted back into world of music and dance. Being snug inside a pipe could have its drawbacks and having a fizzing coconut dropped on top of you highlighted this.

Struggling to wake up and cope with a pressing weight was proving difficult when the whole world around him began to vibrate and hammer him with noise and smoke.

Cuthbert sat on top of the rocking tractor. Nothing had changed since the last firing, so he sat vibrating wildly as the pressure built up in the pipes.

At last the pressure defeated the weight of the object and the first coconut left the tube in a blur of smoke and feathers. Cuthbert thought about this briefly but soon watched the rest of the firing sequence instead. The devices had left clear curving smoke trails in the clear sky, and Cuthbert switched off the ignition.

Percy stood watching, and as soon as the silence allowed, said, "Watcha doin'?"

Cuthbert looked down guiltily. "Sorry, Percy. I just want the Valley back to how it was."

Percy reached under his cap and scratched his head. "Without the people, you mean?" he asked, puzzled.

"No, of course not," replied Cuthbert. "Why do you say that?"

Percy looked at his finger as if surprised that it had survived the world under his cap, and said, "Well, most of the Valley is in the cinema watching a special première, 'Die Messy 4'. Looks as if it's the most realistic one yet, or it will be when that lot lands on them."

Cuthbert stared, then he blinked and stared some more. "They can't be," he spluttered. "This is the gap between shows when they clean the place up."

Percy was definite "They did the cleaning last night, ready for an all day showing. Everybody's there."

In the distance, a dull 'thump' came to them on the wind, followed by others at regular intervals. Smoke began to rise on the horizon and Cuthbert's heart sank.

He murmured, "We had better go and help," as he switched on the tractor. The engine lumbered into life, but was still up on blocks, as Cuthbert revved the engine in frustration. To his horror, the tubes fired another salvo of coconuts, each one following the trajectory of the first ones.

Switching off, he yelled to Percy, "How did that happen?"

Percy shrugged. "They must be the ones I put in this morning. I was going to watch the film before I fired them."

They both set off at a fast run to be of whatever help they could and to see if enough people had survived to form a lynching party. Between gasps Cuthbert asked Percy why he was going to fire the tractor again.

In between puffing and gasping, Percy replied that, "The Valley just isn't the same. I tried to tell one of my stories last night and no-one listened. Can you imagine that?"

They both collapsed in a heap at the cinema entrance and peered into the smoke funnelling out into the sky as they tried to breathe normally again. An angry crowd was milling about in the foyer and began to move out into the open air to escape the smoke.

Cuthbert saw a circle of yellow helmets surrounding Aunt Liza and Anita as the complaining throng forced them outside. Everyone was demanding a refund and someone was waving a stunned crow about. Every time he swung it, another feather fell off.

"This is the culprit," the man was shouting. "Came straight through the screen and set fire to the electrics."

The crowd took up the cause. "Ooh, the electrics," they muttered. Electricity was not really understood in the Valley and could be cited as the cause of, well, pretty much everything really.

"Why can't we have our money back?" shouted someone at the back.

"Because you paid to use a seat and you've used it," shouted Liza over the daffodil ring of her protection.

"What about the insurance?" asked someone else.

Liza was heard to say, "We're not insured against Acts of God."

"Acts of God?" screamed the man. "Don't you think he would send someone a little more impressive than this?"

A few more feathers drifted down as he shook the crow furiously. The crow had suffered enough for one day. He uncrossed his eyes and pecked the man's nose viciously.

The man yelped and dropped him as he flapped valiantly with too few feathers and hit one of the yellow-hat donned hulks between the eyes. The man threw a punch at the unseen assailant and everyone joined in.

The crow escaped the mêlée with a strange lop-sided flight to freedom as, below him, civilisation came to an end over a refund.

'Story of the world,' thought the crow as he gained height. Tales had been passed down the ages during the whole history of crowdom. His ancestors had witnessed the turmoil of humans many times and all the big conflicts had been caused by refusing a refund, usually in a gentleman's outfitters, for some reason.

Cuthbert and Percy watched as the situation developed into a rout as Liza and her crew retreated and the locals started to remove the seats they had apparently paid for.

The flames had pretty much burned themselves down as most of the place was built from materials that even fire couldn't recognise.

The foyer was like an emergency dressing station after a battle. The Valley-mafia was distributing free refreshments from the cinema stock. Everyone agreed that ordinary stuff did taste better when it was more expensive, and the descriptions of actions and injuries was keeping everyone enthralled.

The various groups gradually became silent as a gentle but insistent clicking sound made itself heard. Nanny was knitting at speed, and one of the twins was whispering a translation into his mother's ear.

The clicking stopped and Margery cleared her throat. "I think I speak for everyone when I say that Cuthbert was right. The Valley does not need this cinema. They have no interest in us. They just want to use the cheap land to make money from everyone for miles around. I vote that we boycott this place until they give up and go away."

Everyone cheered and they all relaxed into groups. Some sat on the seats they had unbolted but most sat casually on the floor.

As the conversation died and a restful silence fell, Percy could be heard to say, "My family were no strangers to conflict, you know. One of my ancestors was a Fletcher. That's the name they gave to the man who put the feathers onto arrows, you know. Well, one day, they sent him some bent arrow shafts and his apprentice put some feathers on them without noticing.

When my ancestor saw them, he was furious and he fired one at the apprentice in disgust. Everybody was amazed when the arrow flew away and then came back. He experimented over time and perfected an arrow which would come back every time.

Now, the King was up North fighting the Vikings, but when he came back to fight the Normans who had just invaded, my ancestor had a batch of the arrows ready for him. The King was delighted because now, if an arrow missed, it would come back to be shot again and they wouldn't run out.

My ancestor was placed at the King's right hand during the battle as an honour to his skill, and he handed a bow and arrow to the King. The very first returning arrow was fired by King Harold at the battle of Hastings."

Percy nodded sagely as he finished, and Cuthbert smiled. The Valley felt more normal already.

THE END

About the Author

Patrick Barrett is a sixty year old ex-miner from Mansfield in Nottinghamshire. He is married to Paula and between them, they have several children. 'Shakespeare's Cuthbert' was his first book, though he has been writing comedy for several years.

His aims as a writer are 'to be successful and make people laugh by providing them with an escape from the harshness of real life'.

His other abiding interest is in antiques.